LONG RIDE TO NOWHERE

LONG RIDE TO NOWHERE

William A. Luckey

GUNSMOKE

This hardback edition 2009
by BBC Audiobooks Ltd
by arrangement with
Golden West Literary Agency

ISBN 978 1 405 68278 7

British Library Cataloguing in Publication Data available.

Printed and bound in Great Britain by
CPI Antony Rowe, Chippenham and Eastbourne

To Kate, Rob, and Bill

Preface

This book is fiction; names and incidents are the product of the writer's imagination. However, some of the occurences revolve around the history of the times, and the city of Tucson in the Territory of Arizona.

General George Crook was stationed in the territory from September 1882 to April 1886 with express orders to bring a solution to the escalating Apache problem, and Geronimo in particular. Crook chased and finally met with Geronimo, and convinced the Indian leader to bring his people back across the American border to the reservation. At the last moment, a whiskey peddlar, some say a man in the service of the infamous and undocumented 'Tucson ring,' fed whiskey to the Indians and convinced them the soldiers would slaughter them all if they crossed the border. The Indians fled back into the wilderness. Crook was replaced in early April of 1886 by General Nelson A. Miles, and, after seeing some seventy-five peaceful Indians shipped back east by train, left the Tucson area.

George Crook was an independent soldier. Usually dressed in a flat straw hat and canvas jacket and pants, and riding a mule, he was often taken for anything but the commanding officer. At one point, he was offered a job skinning mules for his own company by a man who had not yet met his employer. Crook rarely took advantage of the comforts given an officer in the field, but chose to eat and camp in the same manner as his men. His presence in the desert south of the San Pedro river at the time of this book is quite possible.

William A Luckey

★ Chapter 1

"So, Marshal. What have you got in your fine hotel for me this morning."

The soft voice intruded into the morning chill of the small office. Lambert Dawson allowed the smallest of smiles to break his before coffee sulks. His hand stopped in midair and he turned around very slowly, allowing a grin to build inside him.

The smile widened to put a gleam in the dull hazel eyes, set close in the long face. "What makes you think I got anyone locked up in this establishment simple enough to head out with you this trip? Word's out, mister. All I got is a two-bit horse thief, a drunk, and a hoorawing cowhand." Dawson paused for effect, letting a puzzled look contort his face. "Come to think on it, any one of them's good enough to ride for you."

The two men watched each other; the lawman's long body bent deeper in its stoop to search the face of the smaller man. His visitor stood just inside the office door. Below average height, he was dwarfed by the height of his friend. The man was leaning against the frame of the door, his hands and face stained a walnut brown by sun and heritage, his strong jaw softened by the graying fringe of a beard. His dark eyes glittered as he worked over the people offered by his friend. There was a difference to the man beyond his darkness: a line of color down the hard woolen pants, an extra width to the hat brim touching his thigh, a belt hammered of etched silver discs.

"Ah, yes. The Señor Maldinado, it is my greatest pleasure," the marshal said as he leaned over in a grand, sweeping gesture to bring the smaller man inside. His reward was a wide grin as the man passed his bowed head and went directly to the small stove and hissing pot. There was no jingle to his steps; his feet were cradled in soft half-boots unadorned with roweled spur or fancy inlay.

Rafael Maldinado poured the two cups of coffee, taking a moment to blow out the dried bug inside one cup. Lambert Dawson took the offering and grinned at his compadre. They went back a long time together. The cups were raised in silent salute. Then both men took their first sip, and winced at the scalding bitter burn. Two sighs came in unison, and they chuckled, the sound growing louder at the pleasure of the moment. It was Dawson who spoke first.

"Heard you was out to the Figured S this time, did some good trading. Word out you brought enough men this time, planning on taking the herd back tomorrow. So's I heard. Got enough beef to feed an army."

Rafael nodded. "Indeed that is what we are doing. We are chasing the Indians again, the cavalry has come in to settle them, and so we must feed them. I must return quickly to my family."

They settled into an easy silence. The visitor raised his eyes above the steaming cup, smiled at the usually talkative marshal, and tilted his head in question. Dawson grinned and continued his ramblings.

"Ole George Ryder, he says you finally got him to part with that fancy mare you been wanting. And she just dropped herself a fine he-colt. What you need with another high-blooded bronc makes no sense to me." He sighed dramatically. "But then, I never did learn to figure you out."

"Yes, my old friend, I have gotten the mare. And the colt is a special one. So now I have need of one more man. But it does not sound like your hotel is holding what I am looking for. The mare must be walked to my ranch very slowly, and she and her babe must have the care of a good man. I can only come to you and ask, and hope. You are the one who knows these men."

Lambert Dawson tugged at an ear and looked down to smile at his longtime friend. They had lived in each other's lives for a brief time and had never forgotten the bond. He started to speak, hesitated, and coughed harshly, then spat at the dulled spittoon in the corner. This time he was not sure.

"Just maybe I got what you need. Kid been hanging around here 'bout eight, nine months. Good hand with a rope, better with gentling the broncs. Got more work than he can handle proper. Ought to see him talk a white-eyed snorting son into standing still for a lady to ride. A sight for damned sure.

You say the mare needs to be walked back real slow, a long lonesome ride. Be a good place for this one. Been in more brawls than any one man got a right to. Come Saturday night and I got to go looking for him to pick him up 'fore the others do. Don't seem to start nothing, but he sure enough is in the middle."

The distress in his friend was easy for Maldinado to recognize. "Why do you think, with this unholy recommendation, that he would do the work for me?"

Lambert shook his long head slowly. "Don't rightly

know. Hell of a look to him, makes you want to plant a fist in his nose. But he ain't dishonest and . . . I don't rightly know.

"Anyway, he got himself fired this past week, right out of the Figured S. Stayed working there the longest. Hit town and took a swing at one of the Figured S riders. Then turned on my deputy, broke two 'a Bob's ribs. Took a pistol barrel to settle him."

Dawson shook his head at the memory. "So he's setting right here, waiting for you and living in the last cell. A few more days and he'll get to calling it home. You want a looksee, go right ahead. Ain't got to writing the charges on him yet. Been waiting for you."

A most peculiar recommendation. Not a kind word or good thought, yet Dawson still wanted him to see the kid. Rafael nodded his understanding, and went past his friend to the locked door leading to the narrow line of cells.

The smell of coffee had brought him partially awake, and then the surprising sound of laughter had brought him upright on the hard edge of the bunk. Damn the law for locking up a man for defending himself. He rubbed at the black-and-blue welt above his eye, and winced at the result. Then Blue Mitchell raised his long arms up over his head, clenching his bony hands together in a tight squeeze, pulling against the tightness in his shoulders. The long muscles down his neck and across his back spasmed from the pull, and his lean face twisted in a grimace.

It took him a long time to sit up, to unfold his length of leg and body carefully, to swing over the edge of the cot provided with such care by the law of Beaufort, Utah. Blue rested his head in the comforting nest of his hands, blocking out the spreading light that came from the one high window behind him. Winter-darkened blond hair flowed past his eyes to cover most of his face. He leaned harder into his hands, elbows digging deeply into the corded muscle just above each knee. Damn these hard nights and cold mornings. Damn this whole entire damnable town.

It could have worked here. He was older now, no longer a scrawny kid too easy to pick on, too weak to fight back. Blue snorted through his hands. He had a skill to offer with these hands now, but skills weren't enough. He hadn't learned how to get along with folks yet, how to talk easy and back away without losing himself. But he was always being pushed, men turning their anger at missed throws and lost loves on him.

Goddamn.

Footsteps brought his head up; not the law's this time, not Lambert Dawson's heavy and too-familiar tread. Softer steps, lighter, with a steady cadence that came quickly to his end cell and stopped.

Blue looked up at the intruder and met a pair of dark eyes that did not give way under his stare. He took his own steady measure of this man: compact, dark, certain of himself. Money, too, by the looks of his gear. Soft cream shirt, still clean; silk kerchief knotted in a bright splash of red; fine leather vest; and the giveaway of the silver belt and thin braid. Didn't see too many like this one; sure was out of his territory.

The level eyes stayed on him, probing him, looking deep into him, but without the too-familiar flush of growing anger. The length of time and the knowing dark eyes made Blue conscious of the dirt imbedded in his knuckles, the frayed and collarless shirt stained dark under each arm, the mended tear down the outside of his faded jeans. His own smell offended him. He rubbed at the welt again, then cursed softly. It was an effort not to look away from the dark face. A heat rose in him, be damned the man.

Blue Mitchell rose slowly, never letting his eyes wander from the man just beyond the narrow, barred door. The dark head came up as Blue unfolded, the dark eyes went quickly up and down his six-foot length. Blue knew the man had him now. He shook his head, strings of wild hair slapping against his face.

Rafael knew why Lambert Dawson had this man as a guest every week in his fine jail. And he could guess at the talent that lay in those limber hands, that loose-jointed body. Despite the easy grin that came and stayed on the wide mouth, despite the obvious youth of the lean body, the awkwardness to the long arms and legs, there was a ready look of insolence to the face that would breed its own trouble.

It was the eyes. Heavy-lidded eyes set deep in the narrow face. A homely face that hollowed out beneath flattened cheekbones. A face made younger by the almost white blond stubble of a thin growth of beard, framed with the flow of blond hair, matted and hanging below where there should have been a collar.

It was the eyes: a dark green-blue framed by black lashing, outlined by a startling contrast of white. They carried a natural insolence that would constantly keep the owner in trouble. And yet there was something in this wild-looking young man that Lambert Dawson wanted him to have. Rafael kept his silence and watched the impatience come to a head.

"You seen enough yet . . . Mister?" There was a wait before the title, a moment long enough to draw insult, to bring a flush of anger. The voice matched the eyes, soft, polite, with a cocky slurring that drew blood. Rafael only smiled and continued to watch. The deep blueness of the eyes flushed a darker green as anger built up in the prisoner. Rafael deliberately added to the fire.

"You are not where you can challenge another, my friend. You are at my mercy. So why not listen to what I am to offer and then speak your mind to me. You cannot lose anything but time."

Blue shrugged his shoulders and turned away. Another one who wanted to ride him, break him to bit and spur. Just like that damned long-headed marshal. One stride brought him to the half-full tin bucket, its odor ripening in the beginnings of the new day's warmth. One more step brought him to the coldness of the high-stacked rock wall, the sill of the narrow window that brightened the air just above him. There was silence from the man behind him.

That son of a bitch was right. Blue turned around slowly on one boot heel, and looked back at the man, who waited with great patience on the other side of the barred door.

"What you want with me? Dawson's got to let me out soon enough. I ain't looking for nothing from you."

He caught the escaping rage in his voice and steadied the last few words. The cell grew smaller, the thin metal bars leaned in on him, threatened to touch his back, push at his side. Then the dark faced man spoke his words with a soft knowing.

"But I am looking for something from you. I need a man to take a mare to my ranch. To walk with her and her new foal. A man who knows enough of horses, who will travel slowly and take great care. For this Señor Dawson says you are the man. And I believe him. For this only he is willing to let you go free. And soon."

Blue couldn't stop his snort of disbelief. Dawson had no cause to do any favors for him, to believe in him. Believe in what? His ability to fight? The words continued from the man, and Blue set his mind not to listen. But the voice was soft, and persuasive.

"I will pay your fine out of here, provide you with a good

horse and a pack mule, and will pay you well the day you ride into my ranch. For this only will the marshal let you go so soon. Otherwise . . ."

Blue thought it over. A nursemaid. Must be some piece of horseflesh to be worth the effort of an extra hand. And this man must be in his own hurry or he would be making the ride himself.

It could be another start. The fresh one he thought this town held for him. A long ride alone to a new land where some didn't even speak his own brand of language. A chance for him to get out of this town, this whole damned state. He'd had enough fights here to last a goodly while.

Before he nodded his acceptance, the dark rancher put his hand through the bars. The tapered fingers were clean, the nails trimmed, but there was a buildup of callused padding at the base of each finger and across the palm. This was a working boss.

"I am glad you will be riding with the mare." The small hand disappeared in Blue's long one, the dark skin a contrast to the reddened and cracked knuckles, the faded yellow coloring of last summer's sun. But the strength in the hands was equal.

"I am Señor Rafael Maldinado. And you are called?"

"Blue. Blue Mitchell."

"Ahhh." The word was drawn out to a long sigh. And the dark eyes went over him one more time. Finally, they came to rest on the homely face, holding the gaze of the strange sea-blue eyes.

"Yes, you are the right one."

The señor was gone before Blue got to his own questioning. He watched the set to the back, the easy horseman's walk, as the man disappeared through the door to the office. Then Blue took the one step that brought him to the tin bucket to relieve himself. The slow grin stuck to his face. He was on his way out of here.

Lambert Dawson was a fair man, as the law went. So it seemed to Blue. Breakfast always arrived before the town got to moving on its own. The board that served for a bed these past four days would now become his table. Blue was hungry. He was always hungry.

His grin widened. From the shape of this morning he would be out of here soon, and with the pocket jingle to buy his own meals. But he still wanted his morning grub. A growing boy needed his eats. And by his reckoning, his birthday was coming up in the next few days. Might even be close to twenty-one by now; never would know for certain. His age changed often when he was a boy, depending on how useful it could be. But he knew the date. April 9. That was one certain thing he did know.

★ Chapter 2

Blue was careful. Two steps out the door and the sun hit his eyes, took away his sight, and blinded him to the tipping of the walkway. He stopped then, and waited until his eyes adjusted themselves to the noon sun. The cold was still there, coming down from the snow-peaked mountains, but the sun was reaching for height now, and he had been locked up for four long days. He blinked twice more, and stood, watching the almost-deserted street.

The voice came from right behind him, and Blue clamped down on the impulse to spin around, his hand automatically reaching for the pistol not yet back on his hip. He thought he'd left the law back in the small heated office. But Lambert Dawson wasn't letting him get away that easy.

"There's a horse for you, down to Pat's livery. Talked to Pat and he'll give you a horse with no trouble, if you don't mouth off. He's had enough of you, like the rest of us. The Señor'll be waiting out to the Figured S. You hear this boy. By God, you better be to the ranch 'afore supper, or the whole town'll be out as a posse after you. You hear me?"

Blue liked the anger rising in the law's slow voice. He

turned his head just enough to see the sorrowful face of his jailor.

"I hear you, Marshal. You worried I won't get out of your town fast enough. Not much can happen from here to the livery, and there you got Pat on his best behavior. I'll be out and gone soon enough. You bet."

"You watch it with Pat, boy. He never forgive you for the paint mare you sold him lady broke. Damned near to kill him. So watch yourself and get a move on."

Blue only shook his head and walked carefully to the edge of the walk, then turned one more time to grin at the law before stepping off into the muddy street.

Dawson watched the long figure amble crossways to the shabby livery barn. He shook his head in despair as a rider had to swerve to avoid running the boy down. Trouble even walking across a goddamn street. He waited several long minutes, then sighed with relief as he recognized the swaying body on the high-headed bronc coming out of the wide-open livery door. Guess Pat had eased up on his temper for this last meeting.

He sure hoped to hell his judgment of the kid wasn't wrong, that was something to him. Hell, even the town curs took to following the youngster on his Saturday night lonesomes. He was hoping Rafael could rope in the wildness, turn it to something good on that ranch of his way down there in the desert. Dawson shook his head mournfully one more time. Sure hoped the kid worked out.

The livery horse wasn't worth stealing, but the idea picked at Blue's mind. The animal fought every stride, pitching and pulling to run. His meager gear had already been tied to the back of his old hull, waiting only for his appearance to be tossed over the back of the rank grullo. Not worth stealing, but he'd be damned if he'd do anything more than cut the horse loose and let it run. His head ached and he wiped at the blood crusting in the corner of his mouth. Pat had gotten in his last few licks. He should have known better than to trust the lawman's word.

The sun felt good, the air smelled clean, even the roll and pitch of the eager horse was a relief, loosening his muscles, clearing his head. Blue pulled his hat free and slapped the bronc on the shoulder as he dug in his heels. The grullo bellied down and bolted the quiet street, leaving scattered streaks of mud and surprised faces as a final salute to Beaufort, Utah from Blue Mitchell.

Rafael was impatient to head out, to get back home before much longer. The cattle were road-branded and ready. They were heading out now, and he, too, would leave today, trusting the high-headed brown gelding he rode to take him hard and fast to the mountains just to the east of the city of Tucson. Rafael's nerves kept his hand too tight on the bridle, and the brown spun in a tight circle against the unaccustomed stinging in his mouth. The Indians were off the San Carlo reservation. It was time for him to ride home.

He let the brown gelding run and brought the horse in a wide circle back down the sloping hill to the Figured S headquarters. There was a horse coming fast, on the north road that led to the town of Beaufort. The brown slid from his run to a smooth stop, settled and stood quietly. Rafael crossed his hands on the low horn of the saddle, leaning on the heavy swell.

His dark eyes narrowed as he watched the wild run of the livery bronc, and he swore softly to himself as the grullo slid into the yard, front legs high, mouth wide. The boy was down and at the cinch before the horse was on four legs. Two quick tugs at the old hull, a pull at the slip eared bridle, and the grullo was free. Before Rafael could speak up, the rider slapped the bronc's shoulder with the sweated blanket.

The grullo kicked out at the wavering shadow, then found his freedom and fled from the corrals, headed out to the open grass.

"That was not your horse to turn loose." The long body of the boy twitched slightly at the words, but the sullen face gave no more acknowledgment than that small gesture. Rafael pushed the brown gelding closer to the high shouldered rider, and spoke again.

"That was not your horse to free."

Blue swung around fast, spooking the brown, sending the fine head back into the rider's hands.

"You can take that crowbait out of my pay. Then he's mine to set free."

There was a sharpness to the words that brought Rafael one step closer to look at his new hand. There was a fresh cut at the corner of the wide mouth, a spreading bruise across the cracked knuckles of the right hand, and a wildness to the vivid eyes that told its own story. But Blue Mitchell said nothing more, only stood with feet planted wide apart, patched gear in one hand, watching the new boss. Rafael sighed and let it go.

"I will show you the mare. And her colt. Come with me, and we will settle you with your supplies and I will show you the map that takes you to my ranch. You must not hurry on this ride, but you will travel steady. Give the colt a chance to toughen up, but with much care. And much thought for your charges."

Blue dropped the gear against the barn wall and willingly settled into stride alongside the smaller man. He was puzzled; the challenge had not been taken. It had not been ignored, or hidden, but put aside as if unimportant. Guess he now owned a grullo mustang running somewhere in the plains beyond Beaufort. He grinned; this was not a man to bristle and strut like a barnyard bully. Blue glanced down at the man who was his boss. He walked one stride ahead of

Blue, talking in that soft and insistent voice, telling him of the breeding of this fine mare, of the perils of the long trip into his country. It was easy to hear the words and let them wash away the residue of anger. Blue quickened his stride to keep pace as they came to the corral.

She truly was a fine mare. About 15 hands, good chested, a rich seal brown with heavy dapples showing through her rough-shed winter coat. A strip of white bisected the clean head, wider at the large eyes, tapering and ending in a diamond above the thin flare of nostrils. Hard legs, short bone, clean and tight with a good forearm and sloping shoulder. The foal was a bright chestnut, clean-headed like his dam, but already carrying the hint of size and breadth she lacked.

Blue stopped inside the pen gate, then slid down the post at his back slowly, making no move that would spook the colt or worry the mare. He forgot about the days in jail, the dark weal spreading across his temple, the foul words and the sting of the quirt that had ended his dealings at the livery. That was all behind him.

Soft sounds came from his throat, muttered soothing sounds that brought the tiny ears of the foal to stand straight. The mare slowed her chewing of the fine timothy hay, and stood quietly, one errant strand of the faded green grass hanging from her soft lips. Blue stayed on his heels. Slowly, one hand came up from his thigh to turn palm up, fingers wiggling slightly. He did not notice the Señor walk away from the fence to stand inside the barn. He did not see the riders come in from the long fence line. He sang softly, mindlessly, head down and eyes half-closed, demanding nothing and waiting for the shy colt to take the first step.

Tiny lips touched his long fingers and then moved away. Blue remained still. The mare took one step and whickered softly; the foal swung his head and came back to the enticement of the moving fingertips. His short, red neck stretched out; his warm breath touched Blue's face.

Then Blue felt the heavier weight of the mare's step, could sense her standing over him. Head still lowered, eyes averted, he sang his quiet words, hand palm-up, asking for nothing. Then the mare dropped her muzzle to his blond hair and picked at a strand. She tugged and then chewed reflectively, finally dropping the tasteless morsel and pushing against his face. Blue laughed gently, and stroked the flat jowl of the mare. Then he reached beyond her to the soft fuzz of the baby's forelock. Both animals stood near his hunched body and he stayed with them, head down and quiet, humming tunelessly.

"Goddamnit, what the hell you think you're doing, who the hell are you?"

The loud voice spun the mare away from Blue. The colt staggered backward in panic, and Blue fought the impulse to roar to his feet at the hated familiarity of the sound. He waited until the mare and colt fled to the far side of the pen and stopped their circling. The foal buried his face in the mare's flank, butting at her udder, desperate for supper.

That freed him. He whirled and ducked through the gate and without stopping landed head first in the belly of Bristol Adderson. He knew that voice, the loud bullying tone that had made his days a misery on this sorry ranch for too long. Adderson stumbled under the attack, heels digging frantically to find purchase in the soft dirt, arms windmilling for balance.

The rush of weight carried them both to the ground. Adderson was a confirmed brawler; he immediately rolled on his foe, hugging Blue and winding his stubby arms around the lean chest, butting his head at those hated blue eyes he could just see. Blue jammed a knee into Bristol's crotch, but the man twisted easily and took the blow on one large thigh. The round head caught the blackening weal on Blue's temple, sending a shock that stunned. Adderson kept his advantage, and rolled over again to pin the lighter man under him. One big hand found the corded throat, one fist pulled back for a pounding blow.

Blue could do nothing. Pinned by the extra fifty pounds, stunned by the crack on his head, he pried his eyes open to watch the fist grow smaller, then bigger. He closed his eyes again and tried for one last buck to move the mountain sitting on him.

Then strong fingers circled Bristol's wrist, while other fingers dug into his shoulder, finding nerves that pinched and bit hard. A soft voice gave him no choice.

"You will get up, Mr. Adderson. You will leave this man alone. I know you ride for the Figured S, but you will not fight with this man."

Bristol loosened his hand wrapped around the muscled nuck, pushed away from the body beneath him in an awkward motion, and stood up, swaying slightly, body tingling from the unused anger riding him. He looked down at Blue's long form at his feet, pleased with the blood trickling from the mouth, and the swelling bruise on the forehead. Then those hated blue eyes looked back at him, and the goddamn son of a bitch grinned.

Bristol looked to the man who had given him the command, hoping for a second chance.

"You sure you know what you're doing with this one? He'll take whatever you got and more. Wouldn't let him near that mare if I was you."

He shook his head in unreasoning anger. "You the boss, you want this sorry son, you got him."

With that final word, Bristol walked away, still trembling with the energy of the unfinished fight. Had the son this time, too, but Bristol knew when he was licked. If he was riding with the Señor's herd, it was no time to fight with the dumb-eyed bastard. There was always later. Someday he'd get that son alone.

The toe of a soft boot dug gently at Blue's ribs. He looked up into the face of the Señor. Blue's grin widened. A hand came down to him, offering help. The shock of the gesture came and went quickly across Blue's long face, but Rafael Maldinado saw it and wondered that one so young would have so little faith. Then the long fingers found his and Rafael set himself to pulling hard against the weight of the downed man. But Blue Mitchell rose quickly, barely needing the help to stand on his own.

A hand on his shouder turned Blue to face his boss. "You did not need to fight that man. A word from me and there would be no fight. Why then did you choose so?"

"That there son of . . . Adderson, he's been at me since I come in. Worked for Bryer for a long while on this ranch. Adderson always was looking to tell me what to do, reason I quit here. Don't take those words from no man."

"So, my young friend. You have the responsibility now to take this fine mare and her foal on a long journey. Are you going to fight each man who questions you? Are you going to brawl your way south, or will you care for your charges and hold your temper? I cannot afford to lose this mare through your imagined insults. This time you must make a choice."

Blue opened his mouth to protest, then saw there was nothing he could offer beyond his temper and his reputation. Knowing all about him, this dark man was still offering to take the risk, willing to trust him and his judgment. Knowing that put a different set to Blue's temper.

He looked for Adderson, and saw him across the ranch yard, stooped over the water trough, splashing at the dirt and blood. Blue brought his gaze back to the older man who was watching him with such intensity. It was a tough choice.

Several long strides brought him near the man. Adderson straightened up quickly and one hand went to a pistol

newly-belted to his thick waist. He spat out the words from
bruised lips.

"What you want, boy? I been warned off by the boss so
you best leave this. Or do you like your fighting this easy?"

Blue said nothing, only watched the round face of the
heavyset puncher settle into its accustomed sour lines. He
dipped his head to shadow his eyes and put out his right
hand.

"Sorry, Bristol. You was looking out for your job."

Adderson stared at the hand almost as if to count the
fingers, to check for the hidden trick. He looked up into
Blue's face, found no heat in the odd blue eyes, and then
took the proffered hand. The two men shook slowly, hands
going up and down twice. Then they broke apart and
Adderson went back to his washing. Nothing was changed;
someday he would get this one all to himself and finish the
fight. Adderson's hatred went deep.

Blue looked for Maldinado. He saw only quick movement as the man stepped into the big barn that Bryer had let
him use for his stock. Inside, Blue found him smoothing a
double folded blanket over the back of a deep gold
buckskin. Blue's rough saddle straddled the wooden stall
divider. Without looking up, the Señor spoke.

"You will be ready to ride in the hour. This it Tico. He
will go quietly with you and the mare, and not bother about
the colt. There is a mule packed and ready. I have papers for
you, detailing your journey, proving your right to have the
mare. There are clothes, fresh bought. It is time for you to
ride. There is fifty dollars waiting for you, plus a horse of
your choice. And I will pay for the grullo you set free. A
deal?"

Blue heard the words and watched the dark face. Rafael
Maldinado continued to smooth out the woolen pad,
stroking the shiny neck of the patient gelding. There were
words that had not yet been spoken, and they had to be said.

"The fifty dollars and a fine horse are worth far more to you than the fleeting ownership of the dark mare and her son. Keeping them can only give you much grief."

It was done. Blue smiled. No bluster, no pictures of blood or promise of pain, just the simple words. He nodded his understanding and smiled.

"Be getting my gear, want to go over them directions with you. Don't want to be getting lost just the other side of the ridge. Pretty damned shameful."

★ Chapter 3

Three days it took before they got it sorted out. Three long and slow days. The mare tugged and pulled at the lead rope almost to the point of wearing it out. The first day's distance wasn't more than two miles, and the chestnut colt was the reason. Blue had figured on only a few miles anyway, knowing the youngster would tire fast and become footsore. By the second day he was wishing this was true; the colt ran and dodged shadows, kicking out at the slow-moving buckskin. The son was enjoying his new freedom, not knowing there was a direction and a purpose to the small group's traveling. The mare lengthened Blue's arm a good two inches by her pulling, and numbed his ears with her screams.

The mule settled the situation. The big colt tried nursing on the deliberate animal, and received a well-aimed kick that sent the baby sideways squalling in pain and fear. The mare spun around at the sound, half-pulling Blue from the saddle. It took another hour for the mare to settle and the colt to finish lunch. Blue dismounted and tied the buckskin and the mule to a stubby tree. He figured to lean back and enjoy a smoke, then try for another mile.

He was too slow in knowing the colt was done. By the time Blue untangled the mule from the buckskin's tail and gathered the reluctant mare, the colt was down flat and out in the short grass. He swore softly under his breath and climbed one more time down from the buckskin's back. This trip was going to take forever.

He couldn't help but laugh. He had nothing much but forever right now. Riding another man's horse, using another man's gear, even wearing his store-bought clothes. What he did own for himself weren't much for bragging on; a battered saddle, two clean and patched shirts, a blanket-lined coat, and a pair of boots. The rest was the Señor's.

It was looking up, seemed to him. In another month he'd have the papers on a good horse and hard cash in his pocket, more than he'd ever seen that belonged to him. Blue nodded his head once in hard satisfaction. Could be a time for decisions, time for another new beginning. It was up to him; today was his birthday and it was his choice. He decided he was twenty-one now, age as good as any, and the fifty dollars was his first birthday present. To himself.

Blue spent a lot of time sitting under that stubby tree, going over the map, checking the thin penciled line of trails, nodding his understanding at the marks in the margins: places to avoid, ranches that were safe, towns that were questionable. Nice that the man assumed he could read. He could, barely, follow the directions, given a lot of time to puzzle them out. He'd learned to read from an 'aunt' who gave him the basics.

An uncle had hired him out to another rancher when he was probably 12 years old and lying to be 14. The wife inlcuded him with her own brood for schooling, said he kept her ten-year-old in line. He'd stayed at that spread for three years, and then the schooling stopped when the lady died in childbirth delivering her eighth baby. One more year and

Blue had it out with the rancher, taking a beating over the danged kid that dogged his trail.

That had been his last year as a boy. He was tall for his age and he grew the hard way, earning his wages on a big spread running for the cookie, pulling all the dirty chores. But he wasn't hired out by his great uncle anymore. From that time on he kept his wages and was smart enough to ride out of the small Wyoming valley. The old man vowed to chase him down for the cash, said it was due him as the boy's kin.

Blue shuddered at the memories, feeling cold in the high spring warmth. Damn. He best not sit here and wander in the past. He rose unsteadily from the base of the tree, and slapped the dozing buckskin hard on the butt. The even-tempered horse opened one eye and put his weight back on both hind legs, getting ready to move out. Blue swore out loud this time, hands on hips, head tilted back. He let loose with all he knew and more he made up. Took near to ten minutes, but he felt a lifting of the old memories and a cleanness in him. Damn, he wasn't never going back to those thoughts again. Ahead was a whole new life. And the trail he was riding was clear as far as he could see.

One week out, and Blue had enough of the clear sky and wide grass lands. They went on forever. There was enough grub and fixings that he had no need to stop at a town or ranch looking for something special. The Señor had seen to that. And Blue was planning on taking his instructions seriously. When he heard men riding nearby or saw dust coming up behind him, he pulled aside into the brush to let the riders pass, to keep himself and his stock unnoticed. But he sure would have liked to hear a voice other than his own.

The slow, easy walk to the buckskin did him in. Put him half asleep on the wide comfort of the horse's back. Easy enough to slip the reins over the horn, fold his hands, and let the warm sun give him a rest. He nodded, head touching lightly on his chest, body going with the four-beat motion of the monotonous walk.

The mule jerked sideways, the contrary mare pulled back, and the buckskin stopped. Blue's hand went to his pistol, which came out easily from the oiled holster. He raised himself in the saddle, swung around in a half circle to each side, gun following his eyes, looking for something. There was nothing in sight but more grass and swelling hills.

As he settled back, habit made him check the stock. The mare was resting easy, the colt quick to nurse with greedy pulls. It was the mule. Blue looked at the mouse-colored animal and swore. Somebody done some bragging once about these critters being surefooted, and there the damned fool animal stood, one hind foot balancing on a rock. Blue tugged on the lead, but the mule refused to move.

He walked behind the buckskin, cautious as he got to the mule. The big head swung at him, the ears flopping madly, but the beast did not shift his weight or prepare his hind end for his normal challenging kick. Something must have caught a hoof. Blue slipped out his knife, and sure enough, when he stooped down for a closer look, he found the trouble.

The damnedest thing. The hind shoe had caught the edge of a flat bit of rock; the mule must have taken one step with the rock trapped there. When his weight came down on the stone, the mule stopped. But that one step had twisted the shoe. Blue jimmied his knife blade under the bent metal and very carefully worked the bit of rock free. For once the mule's contrary nature did not present a kick, but Blue still stepped back fast as he put the hoof down. This particular mule was more than handy with those hind legs. He clucked at the son and studied the two uncertain strides. That was enough.

An hour later the small band limped to the side pen of a ranch calling itself the Line 40. Said so on the sign up over the shed door. Blue felt like he should keep checking his back, as if he'd done something wrong, and his hand stayed firm on the handle of the pistol. Be unfriendly to take out his ancient Henry, but he wished he had the comfort of its power in his hands.

The place looked deserted. Good. Blue's better sense was getting to him; he knew he never should have ridden in here. Just so damned hungry to hear a voice. And for all its fancy naming, this ranch was a cousin to those he'd worked for so many years. Hardscrabble, just getting by, and mean. Blue expected to see that dirty-faced old man come crabbing around the barn corner. It was time for him to leave. He put rein to the buckskin and started the turning circle.

Until a big man came around a corner, a man whose face and manner eased his nerves. A man well into six feet, with wrinkled lines around his mouth, and bright blue eyes. Older some, pushing fifty years, wearing a clean shirt and britches pegged into knee-high mule-eared boots. Looked something suspicious to Blue, but the words came out all fine and friendly. Blue sure enjoyed their sound.

"Well, how do there son. Good to see company this far out. You just step right down from that big feller and get yourself a cup 'a good coffee. Missus 'bout due to set dinner on the table. Be right glad to have you join us."

Blue liked those words, especially the part about the eating. Guess he was still a growing boy at heart, even if he was twenty-one. He looked around one more time, real quick-like, not wanting to insult his host. There was nothing wrong that he could see, but there was an unrest poking at his mind and worrying him.

The big man slapped the buckskin gelding, barely looked over the mare and colt, and joined in the misery about the mule's twisted shoe. "Can fix that right after we eat, son. No problem at all. Glad to be a help." The sounds rubbed over the worry in Blue's mind, easing his conscience enough to let him put up the horses.

There was hay and water for the mule and the stolid buckskin in two piles at a hitching line, and an empty pen for the mare and foal. It was a high-walled pen, shaded at one end, with a hayrick holding the sweetest hay Blue'd seen in a long time. Just waiting there for the mare and foal. He shook his head and followed the big man into the house.

Dinner was waiting there, spread out on a long table almost too pretty for speaking. More food than he'd seen in a long time. The women, they were pretty, too. A wife, so it seemed to Blue, and two girls younger than him. One of them had a wall-eyed look, and the other stared at her feet, but they were young and clean, and smelled pretty to Blue.

The introductions never got to names for the women. "I be Noah Carlson, son, owner of this Line 40. Runs all the way down into the Territory. Good land, good graze. And you be . . . ?"

Blue made his manners as fast as he could, wanting to get to the eating. But the old man made to bow his head in prayer and talk on about their new friend and their multitude of blessings. The wall-eyed daughter had the advantage. Blue couldn't tell if she was looking at her folded hands or sideways at him.

The meal didn't last long enough. When it looked like there wouldn't be enough for all to eat, the women stopped, pushing their plates away in unison. Blue made a choking protest as the old man laughed and handed him another biscuit. Blue didn't have the heart to disappoint him.

The old man could talk. He rambled on about his land, about the stock he planned to raise, the fast horses and wild times of days gone by. He finally got to asking the question

just as Blue was getting into the last piece of dried apple
pie.

"That there mare you hauling along. She's something
fancy, 'pears to me. Easy to see she got good blood in her,
and the colt's a good one. What you doing with them. No
offense meant, but you look too young and down on
your . . . hell, you know what I'm saying. To own quality
stock like them two."

Blue knew better, but the heavy settling of the dinner
meal and the luxury of fresh milk and sugar sweetening in
his coffee shook loose his tongue and gummed up his
judgment. It had been a long time—considering his past, a
real long time—since he'd sat to dinner with nice folks and
talked. And he was beginning to like the looks of the wall-
eyed girl.

He spoke for a long time about the mare and his trip
south. Made it sound like something wild and dangerous.
He kept glancing at the wall-eyed girl and never really
looked into the wide and friendly face of his host. Never
saw the greed shine free in the twinkle of the blue eyes. He
was enjoying the full feeling, the lethargy of a good meal,
and the enchanting sound of his own voice.

The two men stepped out to the front porch, "to have a
smoke, don't want to bother the Missus none while she's
clearing the table." The buckskin and the mule were done
with their dinner, but the mare was still working at her pile,
a periodic lift and fall of the stumpy tail the only sign of life
in the sleeping colt at her side. Blue leaned against the post
supporting the sagging roof, worn out from the food and the
talk. His elbow skidded off the rounded post, and he
stepped forward to catch his balance.

Something shattered beside his head and he spun around,
instantly knowing what was wrong, instantly back in the
brightness of the world. The gun at his side came easily into
his hand and settled waist-high and cocked. But the big man

was fast and took another swing at Blue before he fired. Blue ducked down and drove himself forward into the exposed belly of his host. The axe handle thumped across his back but his charge put both men to the slatted floor. The big man rolled on him, ready to use his weight to keep Blue pinned. A knee to the crotch and two fingers jabbed into one eye loosened the grip, and Blue finished the roll, to end with him riding the full belly and cursing a wild streak.

He brought his right hand around in an arc, the pistol clenched in his fist. The big man tried to break his hold by bucking madly, lifting his butt and belly off the floor in desperate heaves, head rolling madly in frustration.

Blue was aiming for just above the left ear, but the big man's thrashing brought his head up and twisting to catch the gunsight squarely in the left eye. Blue heard the crack of bone, felt the scream start in the wide chest and tear through them both. The body went limp, the big hands let go their hold on Blue's throat and went to cradle the bloody face. Dark lines came from under the double-pressed hands, streaming into the man's wide open-mouth, running down his left arm and staining the snowy whiteness of his sleeve.

It was more than Blue had meant, more than the man deserved. Blue leaned to his left and grabbed at the post, pulled himself off the rocking body. He'd surely blinded that eye, tearing it and drawing out the fluid. There was a milky-white line mingling with the streaks of darkening blood.

Blue made it across the yard, patted the buckskin on the dark gold of his shoulder, and dropped to his knees to vomit. He was there a long time, holding to the quiet horse's leg, body frozen in a mockery of prayer. Voices from behind him told the story: high sounds of keening panic, low murmurs of comfort. The women left him alone in his private misery.

Some time later, perhaps thirty minutes, perhaps more,

Blue pulled himself erect to bridle the gelding, tie the mule to the long black tail, and go to the mare. He would have to do something about the mule's hoof, to bend and reset the shoe. What he should have done earlier, instead of taking the crooked shoe as an excuse to seek out company. It would be a long time before he would welcome the sight of another human. Not until he reached the ranch way to the south of here.

★ Chapter 4

The scent carried on the wind and told him what to expect before the buckskin made the turn around the leaning rock and dropped to the unexpected lushness of the small water hole. Blue felt tension come to the stolid horse as the gold neck came up, the black tipped ears pricked to touching. His own body stiffened in instinctive response to the warning smell.

Smoke. Harsh, acrid smoke with a tang foreign to his mountain senses. Everything down here was different. Hadn't started out that way up at Beaufort, but the last week saw the high grasses give way to growths of tough pointed bush, wide-spaced clumps of brittle brown grass, narrow spikes of sharp-branched trees. The heat had come, too, roasting him under his winter hat, sticking the flannel shirts to his back and turning them black under his arms. Even the small canyons and flat plateaus were different.

But he knew the taste of smoke in the air meant men, and they would be no different. Back ten miles or so he'd made a bad choice and was stuck with it. Still spooked by his ride into the Line 40, Blue had tacked around a ranch and missed a well-traveled road which, on the map, looked to head between two mountains. And got himself trapped in country unmarked by the Señor. Three days he'd been working his way down the rough land, skipping over the crumbly, orange-streaked rock, going wide around the spindly stalks of cactus. Twice he had to stop and pull a long spear from the colt's flank, but now it looked that the baby had learned to keep his distance.

Blue didn't like it. The smoke smell was straight ahead, and the only path he found to bring them out of the endless hills was high walled and narrow, penning them in till the bottom. He could see the beckoning green long before they had reached the small canyon, but the ride to it was a half-day's trip. And now, at the bottom, there was the smoke.

The pack mule was ten lengths behind him, placid and unmoved by the nearness of the greenery, the shimmer of water. But the mare was restless, pulling close to Blue's knee, shoving into the buckskin's shoulder. The colt's curiosity was getting to her. The chestnut was hidden under the massive gold neck of the patient buckskin.

Distracted by the smoke, Blue was too slow. He swung the buckskin hard left but missed the agile colt, who was under the neck and running down the remaining jumble of rock to the soft enticement of the grass. The mare jammed Blue's leg, shoved the buckskin hard off balance. Blue let the big horse go to his knees and rode lightly as the animal staggered up against the mare pulling sideways in panic.

He reached for the brown shiny neck and the mare shied at his hand, eyes white, ears swiveling rapidly to follow the colt. Blue cursed her under his breath and touched spur to buckskin, urging the horse against all common sense to come down the rest of the trail in one leap. The mare came in behind and Blue could no longer hear his own cursing above the clatter of the horses. The pack mule leaned back against the rope.

If there was any hope left the owners of the fire had not

heard his arrival, the mare's high whinny drowned them. Now the whole territory knew his whereabouts. Blue kept the buckskin circling in a steady trot and reached back to unknot the mule's tail line. The chestnut colt thought it a great game and stayed just out of reach of his dam, just far enough to keep her at a high pitch.

Finally, Blue halted the buckskin, dragging the mare to a standstill. Worry turned the mare nasty and she snapped at Blue, tearing a long stripe of denim from his pants that left behind a multiplying line of beaded blood.

"Goddamn it, mare." The curse eased the tingle in his leg, but he never raised the soft sound of his voice. Rubbing his hand down the flesh, he smeared the droplets into the torn edge of the pants. Blue cursed again, holding this one under his breath. Then the chestnut colt found he was tired of the game and ready for late lunch. He found his dam and butted at her hind leg, impatient to get going.

"That old bitch got you good, didn't she, cowboy?" The voice spun Blue in the saddle, and he added a longer string of curses to his complaints. Then he settled the buckskin and took a good look.

It was only one man, and not much of one at that. But this time it was one man too many for Blue. The muscles along his neck and back eased some as he patted the buckskin and took the time to settle himself. If only this jasper showed, Blue figured he could handle things all right.

"Mighty nice looking lady you got there, cowboy. You headed somewheres in particular or just out riding for your health?"

Nosy son of a bitch. Blue swung his head side to side, searching for the other man. A quick sweep of the small canyon gave him nothing that was a threat. He focused on the man before him. The long time between his question and Blue's getting around to answer didn't seem to bother the gent. He sat on his spotted horse and smiled.

"Delivering her and the colt to their owner. 'Most there and surely am looking forward to getting out of this saddle, and this heat. Been a long ride."

That was more than he wanted to say but it had been a goodly time since his words had gone to something other than the horses and the disinterested pack mule. Better keep his mouth shut this time and wait the gent out. Blue was getting gun-shy of strangers.

The rider swung his right leg in front of him, hooking it to the high swell of the saddle, and then reached back into his saddle bag. Blue's hand went automatically to the butt of the Henry under his knee, and the man looked up slowly at the quickness of the movement. A smiled came across his pudgy face, revealing even, white store-bought teeth.

"No business for you to worry, cowboy. Just figured iff'n you been riding a distance then you might be needing a smoke. Got extra fixings in my gear. Right here."

Damn the man. Sounded good. A quick tug at the wrong moment from the mare had scattered his makings to the wind maybe eight days back. He'd missed the bitter taste that eased his worries, softened the loneliness. Even missed the simple act of rolling the paper and wetting it, then the extra twist. But another look into the wide, smiling face and Blue felt more alone. Nobody ever offered something for free.

This rider didn't seem to carry too much in height, but he made up for it in the belly riding snug under his shirt and unbuttoned vest. A clean-shaven face showing the beginnings of stubble, gray hair slicked over a shiny balding head, and bright blue eyes almost hidden in creases folded against the sun. Whipcord trousers and fancy high-topped boots, a good store-bought shirt filthy from being worn too long. The clothes took away any menace in the man, but Blue plain didn't trust a man hanging around out here.

"You want that smoke, son? I got me enough here for you and a whole army. See any Indians while you was riding through? You crossed their big trail back there, you see any of them savages?"

The words slid over Blue, the unfamilar sounds echoing in his ears. The urge for the smoke taste rose in him, battling with his knowledge that something was wrong. He touched his tongue to dry lips and imagined the feel of hot and bitter smoke. Smoke. Something was seriously wrong. He shook his head, strange blue eyes flickering side to side. All his nerves told him to run. But where?

The buckskin head rose quickly, the mare took a step away from the sleeping colt, and Blue had that moment to see the pleasure cross the strange man's face. Then he felt the pull of a rope settle across his shoulders, draw his arms useless against his chest. He cursed his slow stupidity, his voice rising with the anger, and then he went sliding over the broad rump of his horse to hit the hard ground.

There was a moment when he could hear nothing but his lungs pumping in his ears, struggling to pull in enough air through cramped muscles. Then he began to sort out the sounds coming from the fat man standing over him. And they weren't good to hear.

"Cowboy, you ain't even dry behind the ears yet. Likely never will be. Can't figure why the almighty Señor Maldinado let the likes of you bring that bit of fancy horseflesh down here. You ain't got the good sense the Lord gave a jackrabbit."

The rising laughter rubbed at Blue, digging the insult in deeper, the more painful because it was true. He fought to come to his knees and reach the red face to wipe out the stinging sounds. He made it halfway, then a voice, somehow familiar, stopped him, left him bent double.

"Quit it, sonny. Ain't nothing you can do now." The rope eased some of its pressure. Blue straightened slowly and looked around. Off to one side he could see the buckskin, grazing comfortably on the sparse grass. The mare was alongside, matching the gelding bite for bite. The outline of the colt was just visible, flat out on the ground, sides rising and falling in sleep. That son could sleep through anything when the urge hit him.

The voice. Blue looked at the fat man, saw the smile, watched the eyes go beyond him. He knew the man behind him from somewhere. The rope loosened. Blue wondered if it was deliberate. Didn't matter, it was his only chance.

The release gave him room. Blue ducked his head into the loop and raised his arms to turn the rope free, then came up in a wild lurch to slam into the still-grinning fat man. The rush of breath gagged him as they rode to the ground. A quick succession of blows to the round face and Blue felt the body sag beneath him. Too easy.

He was right. In the long timeless seconds Blue saw the three animals raise their heads at the antics, saw the foal rise quickly at an unseen signal from his dam, saw the buckskin pull away uneasily from the schooling of his trailing reins.

Out of the side of his eye Blue felt the long arc of the barrel flash beside him before he knew the power of the blow. He was unconscious before he rolled to the ground.

There was no sense of time when he first heard the sounds. Words, curses of hot anger. Then hoofbeats going away, becoming faint, then more coming back. Words, stronger curses. Blue fought to lie still, to keep his eyes closed and listen.

"No good." The words came between deep breaths as if the speaker had worked hard. "Gone, all 'a them. Not a sight. Tracks went down into the wash, caught up in a herd come down to water. Then went back out to the hard rock. No goddamn sign."

"Damn." A boot toe caught Blue in the ribs, raising him and then dropping him. He bit into the side of his mouth and held back the groan that wanted out. Then the toe came again, harder this time, and digging into his neck. He forced himself limp, tightened his closed eyes, drew more blood from his shredded cheek. He could feel the thin trickle slide out of his mouth to spread through soft whiskers. The voices started again.

"One good thing. Them broncs don't know the territory. So they sure 'nough won't drift to the Single M. But I sure wanted that mare's head. Planned on hanging her upside the sign. Let that damned greaser know what we think on him."

The other voice, the familar voice in this alien land, started in. "Well, to hell with that mare. This here's the son I wanted. Got him, too. Nice and pretty, lying there. What you want doing with him now, Vace? Ain't going to just ride off and leave the bastard here."

Blue gave himself the luxury of a small sigh. They wouldn't hear it over their own talking. Something to do with the horse, yet the one man had wanted him in particular. No one down here knew him, but the voice held in his mind. He almost let his eyes drift open.

There was a whisper of sound. Then the voice again. "Best kill the son of a bitch and leave him here. That there daughter of his comes riding up here some days. Let her find the corpse, let her take the word home to daddy."

Blue rolled frantically, but the impact of the bullet came before the explosion blossomed in his head. There was no pain, only a growing numbness in his chest that drove away the fractured sounds and brightened inside his head to shut out the day. He tried once to move against the paralyzing numbness, and thought for a moment he had stood up to the bitter laughter of his killers. Then even that idea faded and he did not hear the two horses as they were ridden from the small canyon, their riders slumped in the saddle, the fat man reaching behind him for the bottle.

Then even the light was gone, and a coldness settled in the small and remote high canyon.

★ Chapter 5

The words stayed clear in her mind. Even as she saddled the restless yellow mare, reaching for the latigo strap and doing up the cinch by feel. It was unreasonably cold in the predawn, and the soft light put a blurred edge to the shapes around her as she moved by instinct through the low-roofed shed. The old mare pretended to snap at her hands when she slipped the high port bit into the already open mouth, and the girl laughed at the nonsense. But the words of her father pushed aside the small moment of pleasure.

"There is trouble, little one. Men who are looking to put the Indian back behind bars, to capture him and move him from his lands. They are angry that we let him ride the land behind us, as if we could put up a fence and keep him out. These men are angry, and their power is growing. They will do anything. So stay out of the hills, stay within sight of the open land and the house."

She could not believe that any threat against her father, anything to do with the Indians, would be passed down to her and her safety. No man would stop her from riding into her high rocked hills. It had come to her to argue with her father, but the lines around his mouth, the flat light to his eyes, warned her away from such folly. Her mother had taught her well. But she would still ride up into her hills.

The yellow mare swung her head and snapped at her mistress's arm, brushing long teeth across the tough leather brush jacket. This morning it was cool, unusual for the first week of the spring month. Celita swore a gringo oath under her breath, and swung into the old saddle without reaching for the stirrups.

It took her little time to reach the sharp beginnings of the hills that led to the Rincon mountains and the great San Pedro river basin beyond. If she rode high and fast before the sun broke free, she could dismount at the small catch basin beneath the trickle of water and see the quick changes of color as the sun found her valley below. There were better and faster horses on the ranch, but the ancient yellow mare had taken her up this trail for all the years of her life, and Celita found comfort in the presence of the quarrelsome animal.

There was only the sound of the small sharp hooves scrambling over the broken rock, the quiet sometimes broken by newly-angry birds scolding her for her intrusion. Celita reined in the mare. There was the still cry of a coyote, an answer across the valley. She forced the mare to step quicker, to beat the sun to the base of the steep trail.

The yellow mare made the last twist that brought them down into the canyon to the coldness of the waterfall. Celita's small body leaned forward in the mare's descent, her eyes scanned the ground. She was surprised; there was much sign of activity, hoof prints, some fresh, and even those of a mule. And shod horses. Few bothered to come up this high, with or without their riders.

Her slight weight was jolted sideways in the saddle as the yellow mare stopped unexpectedly, hindquarters still on the upswing of the track. The yellow head came up and the mare nickered softly. A dark horse turned its head in answer; a foal peeked out from the offside in curiosity. A dark buckskin head came up to stare at the intruder, high pommeled saddle still in place on the broad back.

Someone had lost two good horses and a wonderful foal. Celita's schooled eye quickly appraised the animals, delighting in the clean lines to the mare, the quickness to the colt. The dark mare came forward with eager steps to block the chestnut colt from racing to greet the newcomers. The buckskin only shook his head and went back to stripping the thin grass.

Celita gasped, then cried out. The sound stopped the curious foal who was turned back by a series of bites from his mother. Beyond the two grazing horses lay a body. A man, on his back, arms thrown wide, legs spread, face pale. Blood soaked through the sun-faded shirt and covered his chest and belly, staining to the waist of his torn denim pants, coming in lines from his ribs to drain into the pebbled ground.

Celita spurred the yellow mare in a series of bucks that brought her to the motionless form. Quick to kneel by the man, she saw a black rimmed hole high in his left chest, blood dried in a crusted mound that did not quite stop the dark trickle coming from the wound. She touched a hand to his face and drew back in shock at the coldness of his skin.

She spoke harshly to herself, angered at her childish ways, then put her hand back to his face, to feel along his jaw to his neck, searching for the thin beat that would mean life. She found nothing but the coldness. Then she picked up an arm, fingers pressed tightly to the veins at the wrist, searching again. And still there was nothing. The arm dropped to the ground dully, raising a small puff. No signs of life, yet that small line of blood coming through the blackened crust was fresh, telling her that this one must be alive. He must be.

She sat back on her heels and studied the motionless body. A livid bruise covered the right side of his head and disappeared into the thick blond hair. He looked young, the faded yellow tan of his hands and the red peeling on his face and nose telling her he had wintered away from the sun. The tanned and peeled texture of his skin contrasted with the stark whiteness of his forehead, and made him somehow more vulnerable. He could not be dead.

A black shadow crossed the hard ground between her and the body. She saw that the sun had entered her valley without her notice, and she looked up into the brightness. Vultures, first only a pair, then three more, then four, joined in the circling wait.

She could not leave him here. If she rode to the ranch alone, he would be pulled apart before they could return. She looked over at the buckskin. The mare would never carry double: this horse would have to do. The saddle blanket was gone, as was the bridle, but the saddle and the high roll tied behind it were intact. Surely he would have a rope somewhere, a belt, something she could use to lead the buckskin. There was no rope coiled to the saddle. She could see that from here. She cursed another gringo oath, louder this time, loud enough to send a landing vulture up in flight.

Celita went to the grazing horses with hope. The mare shied away and whickered to the colt to follow. The buckskin cautiously watched her approach, never raising his head from the scant breakfast.

Talking softly, crooning a tuneless song, Celita searched the thin bedroll and saddlebags. No belt, no extra bridle, but a pair of mended woven reins that would be enough to wrap around the golden neck. The buckskin paid her no attention as she tied the old leather around him, but refused to step forward with her when she gave a gentle tug on the line. She cursed the stubborn horse and punched him in the belly. He sighed and followed her to stand over the body.

The girl was just sixteen and of slender build, but she had worked and ridden all her life. It took her ten minutes of rolling the limp form, struggling with her hands locked across his bloody chest, but she finally eased the body onto a waist-high rock. Then she led the curious horse closer to the rock, positioning him carefully to stand broadside. A hand wiped across her face brought the sight of the blood covering her arms too close. She wanted to scream at the warm slickness but she was silent, afraid that noise would spook the already restless buckskin.

The horse felt her fears and sidestepped once, dropping the body hard on the slanted rock. Celita braced it against her knees and pushed and rolled the limp body back to a leaning position, then halfway onto the saddle, feet first. She refused to think any more that the burden was a human being; it had become a problem of strength and determination.

Her calm voice steadied the buckskin, and she hooked one of the boots around the horn, then kept the horse in place with gentle hands and crooning words. She slipped under the heavy neck, hugging the horse's smell to her and taking its strength. On the other side she could grab the protruding foot, balance the leg on the slick leather of the worn saddle, and pull.

She pulled hard and the body did not move. The buckskin shifted against her tug. The body slipped down the rock. She pulled again, then released and pulled once more. A tearing noise came as the shoulders slipped from the rough surface. She leaned into the free hanging weight, digging her heels in for leverage.

The length of legs finally came over the saddle, one boot toe catching her on the chin. The buckskin moved again,

this time away from her pulling, sliding the body further
onto the saddle. Celita felt it herself as the loose-hanging
head slapped against the fender of the near side of the
saddle. It was as if she herself had been slapped. But the
body was settled on the patient buckskin's back. Then the
horse took one step, and the body threatened to slide back to
the ground.

A shirt. Torn into strips she could tie 'it' securely in the
saddle and lead the horse down the steep trail. There were
shirts in the saddlebags. She remembered them from her
search. They would have to do.

To dig back into the scanty gear that had once belonged to
this lump of meat brought the man's life back to her. She
looked into his face one more time. Fresh blood, coming
from under the lifeless corpse, trickled down the saddle
skirting. He had to be alive.

Celita put her ear down to the face, gently turning the
blood-smeared head so she could listen at his mouth. Very
quiet now, almost afraid to hear something, she knelt at the
side of the horse and prayed as she waited.

A short sigh, a faint rattle deep in the throat. She wanted
so badly to hear these things. Celita looked closely at the
face, upside down to her, eyelids half-drawn back in the
gently swinging head. He could not be alive still.

She saw a lid flutter. The thin dripping of blood split and
ran onto the golden coat. The gelding turned his head and
nipped at the tickling irritation, shifting the body in the
saddle, loosening Celita's hold on the arms. She had to
move quickly. The shirt came apart in her hands in wide
strips, and she tied the hands and feet to the big cinch rings.
A few more strips were knotted from the belt loops on his
pants to the saddle horn. It was the best she could do and it
would hold to the ranch. That was enough.

Before Celita mounted the yellow mare, she knelt one

more time to put her ear up against the parted lips, hoping to hear what she thought had come to her before. There was nothing this time. She brought the end of one finger up to draw back an eyelid, and saw the deep blue-greenness of the eyes, blank and empty of sight. There was nothing in this man now, no signs, no stirrings. It must have been her imagination.

The yellow mare wanted to run. Her breakfast of sweet hay and cool water waited at the ranch below. Celita kept a tight hand on the reins and the obstinate old mare settled into a shuffling, quick-stepping walk, head tossing with impatience at the measured slowness of the gait. The buckskin followed on a short lead. The dark mare and her curious foal came along with them, trotting in frantic spurts to get ahead, then resting and grabbing at mouthfuls of grass and milk.

There was no need to hurry. The burden draped over the back of the stolid buckskin was surely dead. Yet something pushed at the girl; something made her quicken the mare's steps the last half mile on the level ground. The brown mare responded as if to a challenge and galloped past with tail streaming over her back, head high, strides reaching for speed. The chestnut colt followed in great bucking leaps.

The shrill whinny of the mare as her offspring found horses in the mesquite pen brought men out of the long, low building. She stood in the center of the high-walled yard, eyes wild, turning and prancing in her effort to keep her foal in sight.

It was this scream that brought Rafael Maldinado away from his wife to stand on the flat dirt floor of the ramada and see the display of his prized mare. The colt frightened himself with the commotion he caused, and sought safety in the flanks of his mother. And there they stood for the Señor.

No halter, no lead ropes, no pack mule, and no buckskin horse and long-haired rider. Rafael felt a sadness, a sense of loss that the wild-eyed cowboy had let him down.

It was his daughter's voice that took his gaze away from the beauty of the mare and the chestnut colt. Julio walked towards the mare with a loop of rope in one hand.

"Papa, come quick. I have found someone. I think he is dead, I hope . . ."

The words stopped, swallowed with tears, as her father reached the yellow mare and took hold of the bridle. Celita slid from the still-walking mare and went back to grab the buckskin. Rafael let the yellow mare go, and she went straight for her single pen and waiting breakfast.

Rafael went with his child. He needed to look only once at the swinging head to know. There was a band tightening across his chest. He looked up and across the blood-stained back to his daughter's face. Her words refused the evidence of his eyes and his years.

"He may be alive, Papa. He may be. There was a breath, and there is still fresh blood. Look. Please. Get some men, get some help. Where is Mama? We must take him to the house and care for his wound. Please, Papa?"

She must know. Rafael nodded to his child and averted his eyes, unwilling to see the hope in her face. Yes, they would carry this one to the house and put him down gently; yes, they would care for his wounds. But there would be no medicines, no ointments and bandages, only the traditional washing of the corpse, the fresh clothes, the candles around his head. And burial tomorrow in a high narrow grave.

Three men stepped from the crowd to work loose the lashing of the body. The dark leather of the saddle was shiny in the bright sunlight, slick from blood soaked into its seat and skirting. Perhaps Celita was right. There must be some life or there would no longer be fresh blood.

Rafael looked down at the gray face, the lips a thin blue line, the eyes rolled back in their sockets, showing only the clear white under half-opened lids. He touched fingers to the left side of the neck, to the spot under the jaw, then to the upturned wrists, crossed with faded dark lines and pale white in the day. There was nothing he could find.

He did not look at his daughter then, but shook his head against her hopes. The men carried the body to the house, to the small back room off from the kitchen, the room that had held others such as this. They laid the body down very gently and left the darkened room quickly.

A woman appeared in the doorway to the small room. Basin and cloth in hand, she walked slowly across the hard, tiled floor to stand over the body. Slight in build, auburn hair pinned up and covered by a dark kerchief, she waited beside the young girl. It was only when she stood next to her grown daughter that the age of Ruth Perry Maldinado became apparent: the thickening at the waist, the tracing of lines at her eyes and mouth, the barest sag to her throat. And it was standing next to each other that the connection between them was evident: the tilt to their heads, the clarity of the hazel eyes, the smudges of freckles.

Ruth sent her husband from the room and leaned gently into her daughter's side, taking the trembling into her own body. She smiled at her child, then took a moment to wipe with the dampened cloth at the streak of tears on the dusty face.

"Celita, you will help me now. It is time you learned. This is the other side of living. Child, come here with me, help me to remove the shirt. You will have much time for the tears later."

Despite her words, she found the tears pressed hard against her own eyes. He looked so young, this one, too young for the killing mark of the blackened hole high in his chest. But she had seen younger men than this brought home with such holes. And much worse. She stopped for a short moment to wipe at her own tears.

And to watch her daughter. Watch her Celita dip a cloth in the cooling water in the basin and wipe at the rusted stains on the exposed flesh. Their eyes met across the whiteness of the flesh. The pity showed on their faces. So thin, with ribs too easy to find under searching fingers, the muscles slack and too close to the bone. The hard use this one had seen, too much for one who had lived such a short life. A muffled cry came from Celita. Her mother only shook her head in warning and dipped a cloth again in the pink water.

There had been no pain. Not yet. He had to concentrate on breathing, to spend what strength he had to force shallow gasps from his frozen lungs. Just enough air to keep himself alive.

He had been taken somewhere. He had smelled the familiar warmth of the horseflesh near his face, had felt the tugging and the pulling, but as if it were done to someone else. Only once had he been able to make a sound, to force air between his clenched teeth and shape words. It was against the tearing in his chest, the pain high inside him.

The noise had echoed hard in his ears, like thunder. But there had been no answer, as if he had not spoken. Then he retreated back inside his mind, barely conscious of the hands holding him, touching him. He knew the sway of the horse, the rapid unknown talking, and more of the touching. Then the cool wetness on his flesh.

The touch of the cold brought him back to trying. A stiff breath forced itself through his jaw, a surprising stab of pain answered deep in his chest. His body suddenly demanded more air, and he drew even deeper breaths as the pain inside him grew and he struggled to resist its growth. Finally a cry came from him, a cry of rage against the building fire.

And finally he heard words above him, understood what they were saying.

"Mama, he is alive. I know it. Papa." The sound trailed off into a piercing cry.

★ Chapter 6

He knew the trip to town was a necessity. He could no longer find acceptable excuses for the empty flour barrel or the lack of sugar and shortening. The hard push of work was done, the cattle turned out on summer range up in the high plateau between the mountains. The mares were bred and settled, the yearling colts cut, the two- and three-year-olds started. There was nothing left that allowed him to remain away from the town.

A surge of anger rose in him. It was his valley, his home for the forty-five years of his life. And now there were anglos who said that they owned the adobe-walled village of Tucson, and that he, Rafael Maldinado, was no longer welcome there. Perhaps even the sick gringo in his own house would deny him access to what he had fought to build. The foolishness of such absurd anger brought a barking laugh from him. The boy was still sick, too sick to do more than sip warm broth and roll his eyes when someone spoke to him. And yet he, Rafael Maldinado, was putting into the innocent youth the bitter actions of his countrymen.

There were still some who welcomed him, and many who

would trade with him. Stevens, Warner, even Brown and
Ronquist. The railroad brought in more goods each trip,
more trading stock that was stiffer competition at lower
prices. So the Maldinado money was good, even if the
name was not. He grinned at the irony of frontier justice.
The railroad these powerful men had fought to bring their
town was now killing them with its cheap transportation of
goods.

Then he sobered quickly. It was not only his name and his
heritage, it was his life that the gringos distrusted. Living
here at the base of the mountains, surviving untouched by
the indios that had terrorized the vast plains of the Sonora
desert for the past twenty years, and married to one of their
own, a young woman with auburn hair and hazel eyes. This
stuck in their throats and kept the words rolling against
Rafael Maldinado. But these men could not hurt him with
their words.

Still, he was reluctant to ride into their town. He could
not deny that to himself. He saddled and mounted the brown
gelding. The list that Ruth had given him was folded twice
and tucked into his vest pocket. It had been several trips
since she had come with him into Tucson. The first soft
insults turned quickly into ugly words, and she chose to stay
at home and keep a rifle nearby. She had good men with her:
Annuncio, who had helped to deliver Celita; and Mickey,
who knew the ways of the indios and could fight the best of
them. She was safer in the hills than she was in the
civilization of Tucson.

The anger crowded his good sense, and he drove spurs
into the sleek sides of the brown gelding. The anger rode
with him as the horse ran from the hard-packed yard,
pulling the two pack animals into a lumbering run. Their
sheer weight slowed the eager gelding, and brought some
sanity back to Rafael's thoughts.

The fourteen miles to town would take him almost until

evening. Then he would give his list to Warner at the
Mercantile and spend the evening visiting with those few
who did not turn away from him. Tomorrow he would be
home by midafternoon. As usual, he chose not to ride with a
wagon and team along the easier route, the beginnings of a
road carved out through the mountains by the miners in the
San Pedro valley wanting their supplies from Tucson. He
did not like the slow encumbrance of the draught team and
heavy farm wagon. He had a need for the steady surge of
the horse beneath him to soothe the constant anger.

Rafael looked back once to the low, slanted lines of the
hacienda, the ramada shielding the deep-set windows from
the summer sun. The tightly woven mesquite fencing held
only a few horses now; his riders were up in the high valley
with the stock. Then he turned to the land ahead of him. A
few more miles at a steady trot, and he could see the high
rise of dust from the road angling in beside him. There
would be the creek crossing, and then the path he rode
would converge with many others to form their own road to
Tucson. Two years past he would be making this trips with
an armed escort, for both Indians and bandits rode the wide
valley. Now he was safe enough alone. For a while. There
were a few benefits from the rapid spread of the city and its
claim to civilization.

But the claims were not enough to offset the fury rising in
him as he walked the brown gelding through the streets of
Tucson. Stores had come up in great numbers, offering wide
selections to the curious traveler. Books, meats, ladies
apparel, goods beyond the necessities. Most of those on the
street barely glanced at him, looking only long enough to
recognize his heritage. Those whom he recognized, who
had once been his friends, frowned and turned their heads,
the gesture acknowledging their betrayal.

Warner's store, and the two other shops on the street he

rode through, were housed in the thick, ancient adobe that had been a part of the town from its beginnings. Rafael laughed. Now the gringos were trying to impose their former lives on the desert city, the lives they had left willingly to come to this distant outpost. He had ridden past two of the new houses. They did not belong: houses with thin wooden walls, wide glass windows rising high above the ground, letting in the killing sun. Houses set back from the street, trying to sit graciously on wide expanses of lawn, trying to tame the dust with green grass. He could only shake his head at the folly. This change in the style of living would cost a great deal, both to the builders and owners of these great houses, and to the land they were trying to tame.

The afternoon was late, and there were no horses at the railing before Warner's store. Rafael ducked under the long tie rail and took the few steps that brought him to the heavy glassed door. He could see only one customer inside, an unfamilar face in a heavyset body. There was no one of importance here to challenge him.

He shook his head against the defeating thoughts. There was no reason he could not walk into any store in this town and buy what he wished, without interference. But he had grown tired, and he did not like to think of Ruth and Celita alone at the sprawling ranch. He would hurry and return there.

Warner barely looked up as Rafael entered, and there was no greeting on the once open and smiling face. The lone customer paid him no mind, poking with disinterest through a pile of dark work pants. It was easy to hand the tall storekeeper his list and turn to go without exchanging words. He expected nothing from the sour man, and did not plan to wait for an insult. He was not prepared for the eagerness of his words.

"I heard you got a sick one at the ranch. Some rider you hired up north, brought down that blooded mare. What

happened, you ever find out from him? How's he doing
now? Talk is he still ain't going to make it. Must be hard on
the missus.''

Such a long speech for the man, with almost friendly
words and a curious interest in their guest. Rafael looked to
see if the other man had a share in the harmless gossip. But
he was gone. So he allowed himself a small shared grin with
Warner, to acknowledge and bring back the friendship of
the past.

"Yes, he is still with us. Almost four months now, and he
is only half awake for most of the time. My Ruth does not
mind as Celita is able to help her now. But she had missed
her visits with her friends in town, with your Rosa. Perhaps
when this trouble is settled . . ."

But they both knew there would be no return. And there
was a double irony in the situation. For the respectable Mrs.
Warner was of Spanish descent, as were most of the wives
of the early settlers. And these ladies lived their lives
completely in their husbands' heritage, aloof from the
working Mexicans.

The brief flare of kindness faded from Warner's eyes, and
an edge of coldness came back to the man. At the same
time, Rafael became aware of another presence in the
darkening room. Warner reached over his head and twisted
a knob on the light fixture, to bring the gaslight up to
brighten the hollow room. One more of the benefits of the
growing city.

"What you talking about there, Señor? We heard about
your man. No need for a white man to be staying with you.
No need at all. Don't want to bother the missus. We'll be up
with tomorrow's light to pick him up. Sure enough, there
ain't no need at all.''

Rafael turned slowly, knowing beforehand what face
would greet him. A wide round face with gray hair carefully
combed over the shining skull, a belly pushing at the one

button holding the fancy leather vest. Vace Yarborough. A man who rarely worked and had more than enough.

And there was a new one standing with Vace, the heavy shape and dirty clothing telling Rafael how Yarborough had found him so easily. He nodded to the thickset man and was rewarded with a flush to the whiskered face. There was some feeling to the dull-eyed man.

Vace wasn't going to be upstaged by his own man. "You listening, we'll take that man you got up there. Ain't enough to let them Indians ride your land, don't need to be put out by some no-count kid. Ain't right."

There was never a direct threat to Vace's words, never an outright insult, but the man knew the combinations that drove the words deep into Rafael without pulling blood. It would do no good to tell Vace one more time that he never had control over the Indians, that no one man could stop them from using the narrow trail along the San Pedro river and through the high graze. It would always be Geronimo's to use, to ride in and out of the desert toward Mexico. Yarborough and his cronies would never comprehend the words.

Rafael turned his back to the two men. "Warner, I will be back to pick up my stores midmorning. Vace, you are a fool with your words that mean nothing. Let me pass."

Yarborough's hands went up in a placating gesture of abject surrender. He knew the limits, knew how far he could push and not get called out.

"Well, now, Señor. No call for anger here. Just trying to be of service. No need at all."

Vace had no interest in facing the proud man whose hand rested knowingly on the butt of a smooth-handled revolver. Everyone knew of Maldinado's reputation, and his temper. This unborn fight would grow in Vace's direction later, on his terms, on his ground.

So Yarborough elbowed Bristol Adderson hard in the meaty ribs, getting a surprised grunt from the slow-witted man. Then Vace stepped back with a flourish, making a wide sweep with his hand and arm. Let Warner sell to the dirty greaser for now. But that, too, would end soon enough.

There were two men in Tucson who would welcome Rafael into their homes. Two men who had come to the growing city when it was a walled village, surrounded by unbroken lands and clean mountains. Now they were no longer men of importance, losing their power and their fortunes to the gamble of the railroad and the younger, stronger men. But to Rafael and his wife, they remained constant friends.

It took Henry Wallem and Bates Weston most of the evening to convince Rafael not to return to Warner's at his leisure in the morning for his goods, but to get out and be gone before the fullness of the dawn. Wallem found the clinching argument, one he knew his friend would understand.

"You heard this nonsense about the 'Tucson Ring,' about some men stirring up the Indians and then calling for help from the government and the soldiers. Well, it ain't just a wild story for the papers to peddle. Someone is making big money selling extra goods, feeding the special troops, outfitting the scouts and patrols. They want this Indian trouble kept going, long as it don't come close to them. They got a case against you, stirring up the town's folks, 'cause it's known Geronimo rides up in back of you. They want your ranch, damnit, and they want someone up there yelling for help loud and clear. You take care now, stay here the night and be on your way come early morning, before that Yarborough gets moving. That'll get you home in one piece this time."

Rafael listened to his friends, heard their words of warning, and thought of his moments with the smiling

Yarborough. He waited out the night, restless and alone in the high feather bed. It was still dark, the high mountains to the east blocking out the new morning sun, when he rose.

The 'Tucson Ring' be damned. Rafael would never sneak around this town again. He would complete his self-imposed rout this time, he would pack the goods Warner promised to leave inside the safety of the back of his store, and he would run from the town this time. But never again.

The two pack horses objected to the early hour, to the high stacking of the goods, but Rafael kneed the one too-quarrelsome gelding in the gut and pulled the rope tighter across the canvas. This time they might have to run part of the way. Running home. It went against his pride, his whole being, to run. Just this one time, until he could know the safety of his wife and his child. Then the town and its bought and paid for anger would remember the strength of Rafael Maldinado.

The brown was as eager as his rider to make the journey home. The horse pulled the mutinous pack horses at an unwilling jog to the banks of the muddied creek. Instinct made Rafael pull up before committing himself and his load to the shallow ford. It was early, too early for most in this town to have already crossed into the valley on legitimate business.

He stared at the dense thicket of mesquite and cactus, bright green palo verde and darker green grasses. Trails split and ran through the wide valley from here. And it was well known that Rafael Maldinado would travel this rugged trail rather than the more level dust of the miners' road.

But not this time. He kneed the brown to the left and put the eager horse to a lope. He could feel the soft rope tighten across his thigh, could hear the noisy bounce of the loaded pack horses as they struggled to find their footing. Once on the narrow bridge, Rafael stopped and looked down along the winding streambed. Back where he made his usual crossing there were two men putting their horses into the water. They had entered from the east, away from the city. It was two men whose faces he could not see, but whose heavy bulks sat deep in their high saddles.

One of them would be Vace Yarborough. And by now the man would be cursing, filling the air with his unused anger. His companion could well be the sullen man from Warner's store. Rafael was tempted to lift a hand in salute to the men, but instead he reined the brown toward home.

He did allow a smile. The sun was reaching to the tops of the mountains ahead of him. It would touch the tile roof of the adobe ranch first. With the early start, he would be home in time for dinner.

★ Chapter 7

His face red with unexpelled fury, Vace Yarborough yanked the slow-moving paint around, slamming the wide-rumped horse into Adderson's blocky dun. His eyes weren't that bad, and in the clear light of the early morning, he'd seen that hand rise as if to mock him in salute. Vace had to admit that this time the Señor had outfoxed him. It would not happen again.

Damn. His temper finally exploded and he started on a cussing streak that got through Adderson's whiskey-fogged brain.

"You think the greaser saw us, Vace? You think he figured what we was after?"

Adderson was good with figuring out the obvious. The sheer brilliance of the questions settled Vace's temper for the moment, and he grinned wickedly at his new partner.

"Yeah, Bristol, the Señor knows something was waiting for him in that scrub, and he was just smart enough to hit the bridge and head for home. We drove him out too early this time, but that ain't no nevermind. We'll get him another time. There ain't no chance to that."

Adderson still didn't understand what the fancy mex had

to do with getting his hands on that runny-nosed kid. In fact, the mex had treated him pretty good on the trip down. At least the trail boss had; old Hack Lightfoot had been hard with the work and generous with the grub. The three-week drive paid him well, and Bristol had enough ready cash after payday that he'd had one high and wide time in the back streets of Tucson. Not a bad town, and friendly people, especially them dark-skinned females in Gay Alley. A few pesos bought him a lot of woman down here.

Bristol dug his fingers into one armpit; goddamn the itching he got now. By God, he'd been flat down when he shoved his way up to the long and crowded bar and tried to wheedle just one little drink from the whiskered bartender behind the long, splintered wooden barrier. Just one little drink.

The barkeep turned him down. Flat. Never mind that he, Bristol Adderson, had spent most of his drive cash drinking through the two days at this here particular bar. Nope, no give to that man, not even a shake of the head. He'd just looked for the hard coin in Bristol's hand and turned away when he knew there would be none. The memory twisted at Bristol's narrow mouth.

Now his neighbor at this here bar, why, he turned out to be right friendly. 'Merican, plain enough, and generous with the offer of a drink. Then the offer of a shared bottle. Bristol liked the man's style. A good man, Vace Yarborough, even with his mean temper and fancy words. A man that listened to a long story. A man to ride with. Bristol eased himself into the saddle. He was set now. Vace would tell him what to do next. He waited for the words.

What was going through Bristol's lame mind was easy reading for Vace. The man was a big dog, eager to do any master's bidding. What luck, to find the man drunk and broke in that dirty bar. The bum had talked easily, almost too easily, going on about his fight with that dumb cowpoke up in Beaufort, the long drive down. And the fact that the kid was coming down by himself, leading the mare and her fancy offspring. Bristol was hurting to get his own back from the kid. Gave Vace a damned good idea.

He was looking for his edge, for his entry into the small circle of the Ring. Some folks said they was made up, that there weren't no 'Ring' to control the politics and stir up the Indians. But Vace knew better. He figured if he took the Señor out then entrance to the Ring and its wealth would be open to him.

Almost had him this morning, and lost him. The bitterness wiped out the pleasure of his musings for Vace. His features turned in with hatred and he slapped his palm hard against the paint's neck, spooking his own horse and setting Bristol's roman-nosed dun to jumping sideways, almost dumping the big lard of flesh. Bristol's rough scrambling to keep the saddle brought a harsh laugh from Vace. This was the best he could do for a partner, the only backup man he had. What made the man valuable was his set hatred for the kid lying up at the greaser's—the kid they'd almost got up in the hills—and the knowing that Bristol would side with him whatever. An easy man to throw away after the deed was done. Didn't want the Ring thinking they had to put up with Adderson's thickheaded antics. Vace was looking forward to the day.

It took Blue a long time of staring up at the dark shapes before he could figure them out. Never seen anything like them before. Long spindly things that looked too weak to be holding up the ceiling above him. Since he was lying down and the long shapes went across the room from wall to wall, crosshatched by wooden beams, he figured it to be the ceiling.

The beams he recognized from the succession of rough built cabins in the high mountain country that he had suffered as home. But he'd never seen anything quite like this ceiling before. There was going to be a lot of new things he'd never seen before.

It was something to ask the pretty girl when she came back. He remembered one time to try and form the question, but nothing came out. No sound, no words. She had stared down at him, watching his face contort with the effort, then put a hand gently to his forehead, holding him back down on the soft pillow.

Damned silly letting such a skinny female hold him down with only one hand. But his attempt at protest brought a bitter pain to his chest and the return of the darkness.

It took him three more tries and God knows how many days before he got enough air in him to ask the question again. And he still didn't understand the answer. Spoke something different down here, thought he thought the girl was talking American. Guess it was mex like he never heard before. Anyway, she finally said it was ribs from some big monster. Still didn't know if it was animal or tree. Or a man they plumb didn't like. Strange country he was in.

In time, Blue began to remember. Those last few days, when the buckskin hit the split in the high ground and lengthened his stride. They'd passed near to one town marked on the map, the town Blue chose to ride around and got lost doing. Crossed the new mining road too. No sign of anyone there. But once the buckskin got into the high pricklies, Blue let him pick his way, long as they was headed west. Been going south too long.

He'd never seen anything like it. The wide river valley lay behind them when they got into a high flat grassland that the horses didn't ever want to leave. Then through a tangle of rock and hard scrambles that brought them to the down side of the mountains. Below, way out below and across the flat valley, Blue had seen a light green that could be graze, but up here was nothing but all kinds of prickly bushes, and too many of them. Ground spreading pricklies that reached out to jump at a horse's belly; soft pale green pricklies that burrowed into the tail. Got the mule to bucking one time, quite a noisy sight. The worst was the barrel-shaped ones, squatty growing things with barbed hooks that really took hold. Had a hell of a time when the mare got into one of those. She liked to tear his arm off with the pain.

There were others almost beyond the height of a man, and higher. Holding out arms at a rigid salute. Barbed too, like the rest of them. Standing on a small bottom, swelling up and out to their great height. Some were half dead, flesh rotted away, ribs exposed just like a man's.

Ribs. Godalmighty. Blue attempted to sit up, taken by his discovery. Those long round shapes hanging over his head were the ribs from the big pricklies. He grinned through the tickle of pain; made good sense to build with what you had handy. And it had been a long sight between any stand of big trees. Had to climb higher into the mountaintops for a sight of timber.

Standing might not be so tough now. Blue swung his legs out from the light covering and planted both feet on the cool flooring. That, too, was different. Not bare dirt, not rough planking, but hard glassy squares. He looked down past his pale shanks to see the startling contrast of long feet and yellowed toenails on the deep shiny red of the floor. Different, yeah, and pretty. Beat swept dirt all to hell.

Standing was the next step. A quick grin came and went at his own expense. Couldn't be dying, not with that bad a joke. He ran a hand across his face and knew for certain that he'd been well cared for. No beard, not even short fuzz, and no nicks or scrapes. Whoever was doing the barbering was good. He shook his head gently and found the length of his mane shortened considerably. No swing to it. Someone was trying to civilize him while he slept. Probably figured it to be the only way it would get done.

His searching fingers rasped across the roughened texture as he stood up into the support of the closest wall. He inspected this wall at eye level, finding it hard to get enough air to stand alone, then realized his chest was heaving, panic building in him. Something loud and angry came into his shrinking world.

A voice, a sound of long skirts, something familiar in this strange world of brown-ribbed ceilings and glass floors.

"Señor, you are not to be up. There is still much infection in you. Please to lie back down and rest."

A hand on his shoulder pushed down firmly, guided him to the easy comfort of the high bed. Blue thought to argue and almost got the words past his open mouth, but a slender finger crossed his lips.

"I do not want to hear those words. You have argued enough. Lie still."

This time it wasn't hard to give in and do what he was told. Small hands quickly pulled the light sheeting up around his shoulders and then sought out his face, touching his forehead firmly, resting there for only a moment, then whisking lightly across his mouth. He looked up into the almost familiar face, and was shocked.

He remembered bits of her from his waking moments. At least he thought it was her. Black hair colored like a bird's wing, shiny enough to have its own light. Strong angular face softened by the improbability of freckles, scattered across her nose and high on her cheeks, freckles that belonged to fair skin and chestnut hair. The eyes were a soft hazel green, like the high pines of his own mountains, not the soft brown or glossy black that lived with her dark hair. Must be confused with someone else, must be another woman here. Not just her.

She seemed to know his confusion. "You are safe here, Señor Blue. This is your home. I am Celita. I found you up at the canyon of the wild horses. And you are safe here."

He liked the name, liked the sound of the words that said he was safe. Something new for him. She touched her fingers one more time to his face, then Blue thought she smiled. But his eyes were closing against his will, and his last thought was of her smiling face.

There were other times when he woke up, other times he tried to stand. But each time hands and his own weakness pushed him back, while voices gave him orders. He gave up counting, almost gave up trying, but he kept the freckled face with the shiny black hair alive in his imagination. One of these times he would make it to his feet and find her. Find out if she was real.

Finally there were days he was left alone to walk around in his small room. The first time, one trip was all it took to send him back to the safety of the high bed. Then each day he could take more time on his feet, walk more times around the closeness of the room, counting the steps it took to complete the circle. One time around, then three times, then almost fifty times.

No one was there to stop him when he finally made it out of the small room back from the kitchen. Clean clothes, a loose white shirt, and soft faded pants had been hanging over the back of the chair for two days, waiting for his try. They were much too big on him but they covered him and that was enough.

There was only an old woman in the kitchen, and she wordlessly handed him a cup of the bitterest coffee he'd ever tasted. And that was saying something. She smiled at his rasping thank you and went back to her chores.

He guessed it would be midmorning. There was no one around outside. Standing under the long shed-row roof outside the door, he could look out over the wide land below. Same view as he'd had on his climb down to the small canyon. A whole state it seemed to him. Flat forever, broken only by the blue edge of ragged mountains clustered in small groups. But the flat land went around the peaks and out into the sun.

It came to him he didn't even know the time of year, and didn't know enough to make a guess. Didn't know how long he'd been here, what day or week or month. Hell, could even be the year, for all he knew. Been spring when he hired out to Señor Maldinado, took about a month for his trip down. Beyond that he didn't know.

It was too much. His mind spun, put him off balance enough to drop the tin cup and reach for support. There was nothing here to recognize, nothing to tell him what was what. God, he'd been shot. That much he could remember.

His breathing came in short gasps, a familiar pain rose in his chest. Two steps back brought him against the coolness of the wall, a solid wall of simple mud. 'Dobe they called it. Now he remembered. The hard man with the gray streaked beard, the fawn-colored pants, and knowing eyes. The cell and then his freedom. The ride south with the special mare.

A wicked smile on a greasy face. And the shot that canceled everything. Shame rose in him. To be so stupid, to be caught out so easily by the grinning man and his unseen companion. Blue's breathing eased, his heart slowed back to a familiar beat. Then he became aware of footsteps.

A man walked through the corral yard, raising dust with each step. His head turned toward the darkness of the roofed area and he seemed to recognize Blue. His path changed course, and Blue came to the front of the low-hung roof line. He wanted to meet this man halfway. He had much to explain to him.

"It is good you are up and about. My wife and daughter will be very happy. They have been worried."

This was his host, and once his boss. Blue felt the shame

return. It took him a moment, but the words came out, roughened by the panic and the need to know.

"The mare. Did she come in? And the colt. Feel real bad about them."

The raised hand cut him off. "You have asked that question many times these past months. The mare is fine. Carrying another foal to my stallion. And the colt is turned out with the others of his own age. They are well, Señor. So rest your concern."

In foal. Past months. My God, how long had he been here? Blue found he needed the wall again, needed something solid to lean on and digest the news. Must be coming to fall now; missed the whole damned summer. The boss seemed to be reading his thoughts.

"It is late now, almost October. You have been with us five months almost. The bullet angled from your shoulder blade, passed through you into the ground, but it almost took your life with it. It is a miracle. The doctor believes it was only the unreasonable chill of that night that kept you from bleeding dry.

"It was my daughter who brought you here, and who has kept you alive. It was she and my wife who have done the nursing. Let us both be thankful for their care."

There was a long pause when there were no words. Blue knew it would take him time to sort out the long months, if ever. But for now, just standing here, feeling the warmth of the late sun sneak under the low roof, was enough for him. He gave his own silent thanks.

Rafael Maldinado watched the young man who had almost lost his life for a horse and an unknown hatred. The insolent blue eyes were sunken deep in the long bony skull; dark shadows rimmed them to give an unholy glow. But the go-to-hell look was still there, and had been the first time the lids had opened. This one had not yet changed.

"What do you remember? Did you see the killer? There was powder on your shirt, he must have been very close.

It was only fragments at first that he could pull together in words. But the beginning of his descent into the canyon, the appearance of the smiling man, brought the day back to Blue with a gut-twisting spasm of fear. It must have showed on his face, for the Señor reached out a gentling hand to touch him on the arm. But Blue shook his head against the kindness and plodded through the splintered story, exhaustion slowing his words at the end.

"Guess they was certain I was dead. Kept talking over me as if I was nothing. About the Indians. Geronimo. Figured to take the mare's head and put it on a post to teach you manners about the Indians. Could hear them as if I was someplace else and listening in. Reckon you know what all that means, 'bout the Indian and all. Didn't figure to please you, finding that head on a post."

The utter stillness of the man came through to Blue. A complete and rigid silence, the breath barely entering and leaving the body. The rambling length of the violent tale changed the man from a quiet and thoughtful listener to a living statue.

Rafael snorted. It had been a warning, a cruel and vicious act meant as a warning. To him alone. But there had been a witness left behind, who now gave him a face that he could put a name to. Vace Yarborough. And the other one with him must be the heavy one from Warner's store. Was Charlie Warner in on this? He eased the tightness and turned back to the young man who had been promised fifty dollars to ride into this feud, and had almost died from it.

He looked closer. There was a fear that widened the murky blue eyes, that put the thin back against the adobe wall. Then Rafael looked even closer into the darkening eyes. It was more than fear, it was a deep trembling, a life-stealing tiredness. A fine sweat on the forehead, a heavy pull to the eyelids; this was exhaustion stealing back from the weakness of fear.

Rafael supported one arm and turned the boy around to the house. Blue walked back into the welcoming coolness. There was no fear inside. That would wait until he was stronger, better; then he would ride with the Señor to find the killers. Blue leaned into the strength of the man, and shuddered at the touch of coldness as the door opened.

★ Chapter 8

Her fingers were better suited to other tasks, and there were other chores she far preferred to the demands of sewing, but a quick glance at Mama's face reinforced the necessity that she do this task, and without complaint. There was no easing to the set of her mother's jaw, no humor in the hazel eyes. Outside there was a special three-year-old that needed gentling, but inside there were shirts and socks and a soft blue flowered dress that needed mending.

"Mama, why do the people in town hate us so?" The words came rushing out of her before she could stop them. And she shuddered at the flare to her mother's eyes. But she did want to know. It had been three months since Papa's last trip to Tucson. Yesterday he had mounted the brown gelding and taken the lead to the pack horses; yet there had been no laughter in him, no eagerness for the visiting. She remembered trips when they all rode in the wagon and stayed two days.

"Celita, there is only nonsense in your words. There is nothing to fear in your father's trip. Child, get on with the mending and leave the worry to those who know. There is no one who hates us, and many who are friends. Your father has business with these people, and with our good friends in town.''

There was more Celita wanted to say, more questions to ask and hope for the right answers. But slow footsteps across the tiled floor stopped her. A familiar face appeared in the doorway.

"Morning, ma'am. Miss Celita." Blue Mitchell stayed outside the door. After two weeks up and around, he had not lost the embarrassment he felt around the two women who had nursed him. They owned an intimate knowledge of him that rode uneasy.

"Ma'am. Thought to try riding this morning, but I be slow getting to the horses. Your riders are gone now, and I don't want to just help myself. Wanted you to know what I be about.''

"Mr. Mitchell, you are not well enough yet. You need . . .''

"Ain't fitting for me to speak up, ma'am, but I best get back to a horse and soon. Been taking up your time long enough now. Need to try myself and get going. Just want you to know I weren't stealing a horse or gear, just going to saddle and ride a spell.''

Blue stepped back and dropped his head in a curt nod, then walked away from the mother and daughter. It wasn't getting easier, talking to these women. He stopped to wipe away the sweat gathering at his hairline. Women. Couldn't meet them two pairs of hazel green eyes yet. More willing to take on them big cactus and a pair of rattlers. Blue moved quickly and found blessed freedom in the dusty outside and the heat of the air.

Thoughts and fears went back and forth between mother and daughter quickly, without words. Blue Mitchell was still weak, had spent too long in bed, and not yet gained back the strength lost to the months of fever. He wore out fast, pushing himself each day to exhaustion. The long and homely face showed the strain. Celita's head turned as they heard the soft sounds of his coughing. Already this morning he had come close to his limit. And now he was headed out to ride.

"Go, child. You pick the horse, you ride with him. Trail him if you must, but do not let him go off alone."

Her exit from the room left a mound of blouses, one long sock, and her mother with a gentle smile to ease the ache of her constant worry. The two young ones. Caught up in their discovery of each other, enchanted with the new world they had invented for themselves.

Ruth looked down at her hands. She remembered her own discovery of that world. Her hands came into focus: nails broken, veins standing out across the tanned backs, skin wrinkled and stained. It had been an instant recognition of Rafael and what he would mean to her. Now it was her daughter's turn.

Even behind those insolent eyes and borderline drawl the boy was courteous in an awkward way, shy and uncertain. As her husband told her, he could be a wild one. Yet around Celita and herself he retreated to mumbled stammering and long silences.

Her hands had a life of their own. Without thought they went back to the details of the mending, leaving Ruth Maldinado with her memories.

"Take the bald-faced sorrel. He's nice and gentle, won't give you much trouble."

As soon as she spoke, Celita knew. Twice today she had spoken wrong. She watched red color the long face, saw the odd blue eyes darken. The words, when they finally came, were soft with anger.

"Thanks anyway, missy. I can pick my own mount. Even

wore out like I am I can ride anything. Ain't nothing can
lose me once I hit the saddle."

She let her own anger come full blast. "I picked up the
pieces of you once, and don't want to do it again. You listen
to me this time."

Blue turned away from the girl. Rope in hand, one loop
hanging from his right hand, coils drooping down his left
side, he walked to the horses. Damn her quick mouth, and
damn her more for being right. He knew she was watching
as he twisted the open end of the rope and let it slip out to
catch hold of a big red bay. The horse pulled back for an
instant, went up, and then came back to stand quiet. A
fighter this one, but a good honest fighter.

Celita climbed the tight weave of the mesquite fencing,
cursing as always at the hooks and knobs that caught at her
clothing. She wanted a good seat for the fireworks, and to
be close when he hit the dust. Half her mind wanted him
punished for going against her orders.

But he was only standing in the center of the pen, rope
held loosely in one hand, talking softly to himself, barely-
muttered words she could not hear. She watched the bay.
The horse seemed to be listening, ears tipped forward, eyes
settled on the tall and swaying young man. It was as if the
horse understood.

His fingers tightened on the rope, tugged lightly at the
bay gelding, and the horse came forward first with one step,
then three, then stopped for another look, and walked
quietly to stand with muzzle touching the loose folds of the
white shirt. Blue reached out and stroked the searching
nose; the bay blew through distended nostrils and Blue's
hand cupped the hot air.

She was fascinated. The tall figure turned and walked
away. The bay horse followed on a loose line. Celita slipped
from her narrow seat and ran to the small shed that held the
ranch gear. She wanted to saddle the yellow mare fast
before Blue got away from her.

His eyes adjusted fast in the dimness of the shed, and Blue found his own gear in the corner. The narrow horn and rounded swell were easy to see among the low, split seats and flat horn of the spanish saddles. There was a polish to the old hull, oiled and smooth, even repaired at the torn skirting and cut away strings. He thought to thank the girl, but her head was buried in the belly of the old mare, fighting to pull the cinch another notch. Her stubborn silence kept him quiet. He was building up quite a debt to these people.

The bay had two bucks in him that loosened Blue. But the big horse did not take the advantage. He picked up an easy lope to follow behind the switching tail of the yellow mare. Blue locked hands on the horn and fought for his balance. He couldn't be this weak, this off-center and fighting for air from the two lady's crow hops. His snort of disgust turned to a dry cough that slowed the yellow mare's run. Celita's dusty face came back over the cantle to watch him. He tried to smile, and bent double with a cough.

His pride hated it, but Blue admitted to himself that the walking was easier; he could find enough air at the slower pace without much struggle. The bay jigged for a few steps and then settled. Blue got his breath in two gulps of air, and spoke to the back of the girl's head.

"Now, how about you take me up to where you found me. Want to see it sitting from a saddle. Want to know how I got back down here."

The reply was curt; "I can tell you how you arrived down here, mister. Slung over the seat of that old saddle, head buried in the buckskin's belly. That's how you got here. And if I take you back up there today, you'll come down the same way. Only this time for a certain burial."

She angled the mare across the narrow path. "You listen. You got your way to sitting up on that particular horse. And maybe you'll be all right. But now you follow along.

There's enough trouble without having to nurse you again. This one time you do what you've been told."

She watched the flare in those heavy blue eyes and stood ready to battle with him. Then the anger died as she saw the weary set to him. And she smiled, to lessen the taste of her words.

"Thought you might like to see some of the stock. The bunch of new weanlings usually graze the day in a small canyon about a half-hour walk from here. It's really pretty. Papa grains the weanlings each evening so they come back to the ranch, but they always end up in the canyon, and you can't blame them. Anyway, I thought you would like to see them. The chestnut colt's there."

Blue had to see it her way this time. He bit off an angry word and eased hmself into the support of the high cantle.

"Yes'm. Sounds good."

There couldn't be any fight to those words. He was almost wrong. The girl looked back at him queerly, then shook her head as if in anger and swung the yellow mare back onto the trail. Blue followed the stiff, set back, and let his mind wander, to feel the heat soaking into him, the loose rhythm of the horse beneath him.

The yellow mare stopped at the first shot. Then a series of shots came, carefully spaced as if taking practice at a target. Blue had no answer for the question in the girl's eyes. They were silent to listen for the next shot, then Blue shook his head. Between the narrow ridges and piled rocks, he couldn't find the direction of the sounds.

Celita knew. She slapped the yellow mare to a run, and the bay came in a leap that almost left Blue on the ground. A ten-minute scramble and the trail opened to double width. Blue dug in his heels and yelled at the big bay gelding, chasing him past the girl on the faltering mare.

The pair leaned into the corner and burst into the small canyon. The bay stopped and went high on his hind legs, squealing in his fright. The yellow mare slammed into the rearing horse, knocking him sideways into the brittle rock wall.

There must have been fifteen weanlings grazing here. Blue counted fast, trying to turn the still-warm flesh into unimportant piles of meat. Most were down and still, blood circling under their heads or showing dark at their chests. There were three still alive, struggling with their killing wounds. Blue went automatically for the Henry that would be under his leg and found nothing. He turned to the girl, numbed by what was laid out in front of him and by what he had to do.

She stood at the head of the yellow mare, reins held in both hands, knuckles white with the holding. Tears tracked white lines through the fine dust covering her face, spotting the white collar of her shirt. Blue spoke her name gently, and she turned her head blindly to the sound. She could not answer his question, but slowly pulled the yellow mare sideways, offering the sheathed rifle on the off side to him. Blue climbed from the bay and forced the reins into her stiffened hands, then took the light rifle and walked to the center of the carnage.

The three still alive were at the far side of the small graze. One sorrel filly made it to her feet to hold a hind leg off the ground, cannon bone showing through above the fetlock, blood pouring from the hole down the white stocking to puddle below the hoof. The filly turned to stare at Blue, then hobbled away until her weight came to the off hind leg. She collapsed, whining in her pain. Blue aimed and pulled the trigger in one easy move and watched the filly flop over on her side.

A thick sigh came from him. The single shot echoed against the rock. Blue heard the muffled cry behind him but could not turn to offer comfort. There was nothing he could give until his chore was finished.

The bay colt lay on his side, blood pumping from a hole behind his forearm. As Blue came to the colt, his breathing slowed, then stopped. Blue touched his fingers to the underside of the throat and felt nothing. He rose and continued his bitter walk.

It was the chestnut colt. The big copper youngster that had plagued Blue for the long miles back in the spring. And whoever had created this slaughter had known the specialness of the colt. For the wide eyed chestnut colt was mutilated, not enough to kill but enough to make his living a hell and his death a certainty.

They must have gone after the colt first, worked on him before the shooting spree. The big youngster would walk up to any man and stick out his nose in curious friendship. Blue choked on the hard breath that escaped through his teeth.

He'd been skinned out from the shoulders back. The hide, a glossy red, was tacked to a mesquite bush. Small burbly sounds came from the drawn-back lips, the wide eyes rolled back into the sockets, the tongue protruded from between the short stubs of teeth. Blue squatted down to the colt and placed a hand gently on the damp neck. The colt was alive, but there was no life left to him. Blue placed the barrel of the rifle behind the ears, stood up, pulled the trigger.

The cry from the girl brought him back. He did not have the luxury of tears for this pain, and she needed him now. The walk back to the neck of the canyon and the waiting girl seemed to take him a long time. It was hard to breathe; his hand trembled on the blue barrel. Whoever planned this had done it well. In, out, and gone, with no witness. And his contempt of the Maldinados a bloody and vicious act. No one would kill this way for sport.

Celita would not lift her head to look at him. She stood alone, fighting the anger and the tears. Instinct made Blue put a hand to her thin shoulder and pull her to him so very gently. Bodies barely touching, she leaned her head to his chest and sobbed quietly. His hand stayed lightly on the thinness of her back, and Blue wondered at the clean smell to her. A fierceness he had never known came over him, and kept him motionless as she cried.

Blue glanced back at the girl as they rode into the stillness of the ranch. He had seen the brown gelding at the tie rail, sweat dried on his coat, cinch loosened to rest. The two pack horses stood head to tail under the scant shade of the shed roof. It was for her to tell her father; it was for Blue to put up the horses and wait. Celita did not look at him, or warn him to take care, but slid from the off side of the yellow mare and went toward the house. Alone.

Blue stripped the gear from the horses and dumped it, not caring about the heavy puff of dust that rose to cover the saddles. He was at his limit now, and he would be needed. The two horses wandered to the water tank, and Blue stayed hunkered down against the safety of the thick mud wall. He could wait here for a while. It was a long walk to the house.

Something touched his leg and Blue opened his eyes to fawn gray pants tucked into black half boots at the level of his eyes. He struggled to stand, then sank back as the soft voice stopped him.

"Just tell me. Were there tracks, what direction? How many riders? Tell me."

Blue found his voice, leaned against the comfort of the wall to push himself erect. Maldinado's pale face came into view.

"Looked to be two riders. One horse needing hind shoes. Split track. Found these shells." He handed them to Rafael. "Must have left just before we got there, fresh manure, fresh blood. Knew the land all right, knew right where to head up and out. Good aim. Hit each youngster with one shot. Betting the filly was last, a hurry up shot 'cause we was coming. But the colt . . ."

Here he stopped. Something took the rest of his breath, and Blue sagged back into the wall. He would not look at the darkened face beside him. The voice finally came so softly that Blue almost thought he imagined the words.

"I will go and look for the tracks, and the men. We will find them and we will take care of them. Celita is with her mother. You will stay here for her."

These were not words to argue with. He watched the man step to the side of the brown gelding and tug at the cinch. An old man on a sorrel and the Indian he knew only as Mickey came from the mesquite corral.

Weakness flooded him; relief at not having to climb on the bay gelding and ride, and anger that there was not more to him. Blue felt the trembling start in his knees, spread to his belly and his chest. Didn't think he would even make it back to the house quite yet, never mind a wild ride back to the bloody canyon.

★ Chapter 9

It was war. He would take only these two men, the ancient Annuncio and Mickey. If there were tracks these two would find the trail and keep to it. But Rafael Maldinado knew who had fired the shots; he would be found in the town by now. Drinking and celebrating his simple victory.

Annuncio rode hunched over in the old military saddle. He'd added comfort to it for his old bones by a double fold of brightly woven rugging. Body broken and reshaped by too many hard falls, he still rode out early and came in late. His dark eyes, disappearing in the years of wrinkles, missed little. The stubborn Indian was willing to walk behind Annuncio, and together they could see everything.

It was Annuncio who found the first sign. He pulled up the high-stockinged sorrel to lean over and point at the one track on the windblown trail. A hind shoe, the toe worn thin to cracking. They rode on, picking up to a steady lope. There was one more such print before they reached the small canyon.

It was Mickey who rode through the formless shapes, Mickey who ignored the great flapping birds as they plodded into flight at his interruption. Rafael found he could not look at the torn piles. Mickey drove his horse up the steep incline of the far wall. There was the hint of a trail that wound back across the slanted wall, twisted, and returned to come out on the rim.

At the wave of his hand, Rafael spoke softly to the old man and they put their horses on the obscured trail. There were no words to speak, no thoughts to expose, about the death they left behind them.

They knew when the trail was lost. It headed south into a dry wash, then out over glare rock. White lines scarred the gray surface to mark the passing. Then the faint tracks hit the wide valley and joined with others to follow the sooted curve of the railroad.

"Annuncio, you and Mickey ride one on each side of the tracks. Follow them forever. And you will find where these two riders changed horses or turned back."

Rafael spun the brown gelding and pushed the horse to a run. He did not want to see the faces of the two men. Common sense made him pull up the brown after less than a mile. He had chosen in a hurry and now he would pay. Habit made him cinch up the brown when he had need of a fresh horse. Hurry brought him out with handgun and rifle and no extra shells, not enough for the war in his mind. He slapped the sweaty neck of the faithful horse and felt the trembling deep in the animal's heart. There was no choice. He turned to the high safety of the ranch.

The trail dipped back into the narrow wash and up across sharp rock to home. Partway up the far side the gelding lifted his head and snorted. Rafael was ready. Three more strides and they came up onto flat ground. Rafael had his rifle angled across the saddle in front of him, hands cradling it gently.

There were two horses waiting. It was Blue Mitchell on a light bay, holding the line to a long-legged buckskin. Arms

crossed on the wide horn, the boy said nothing but he held
out the bridle reins to his boss. Their eyes met for an
instant, and then the bluish-green ones slid away from the
hot anger riding the Señor's face.

It took only moments to pull the gear from the brown and
tighten the cinch on the buckskin. Blue kept his silence as
the Señor slipped the headstall from the tired brown and
sent the horse home. The first strides were a jerky gallop
that settled to a trot. Then Rafael mounted and they rode
out.

"Gracias." The word came after ten minutes of silent
riding, and Blue dipped his head. Maldinado looked back at
his silent companion and waved a command to ride up
beside him. There was a holster buckled to the narrow hip,
butt handle gleaming dully. Rafael's gaze went to the
saddlebags tied on behind. They bulged with sharp edged
indentations. Shells. There would be a rifle on the far side
of the bay, and his own horse would be so equipped, too.

He took another look at this companion of his. The hot
blue eyes came back at him. There was still no softening to
their insolence. Then Blue spoke and the voice sweetened
the temper in the eyes, even with the hoarseness of its
sound.

"Got a pistol for you, belt too. The missus said you
always carried the Sharps. Got extra shells for that. Thought
you would need the fire power when you hit town."

Enough fire power for an army from the heft of the bags.
There was more to the boy than temper and talk. The
horses, for example. The buckskin was a race horse, high-
bred and hot-tempered with a willingness to run. Not a
stayer, but one to make the speed. And the bay was no less a
horse.

Then he thought of the rider, took note of the slumped
shoulders, the quick rise and fall of the lean chest. There
was no time for compassion. The boy had chosen to ride

with him and he would not turn him back. The boy had
made his declaration and Rafael needed the ease with the
weapons, the hot temper and the sullen eyes. There were no
words that would turn this one back.

"Well done. My friend." Blue's head came up at the
words. There was no bite to the sounds, no bitter twist to the
meaning. "Annuncio and Mickey have continued along the
rail bed but they will find nothing we do not already know.
You and I, we will find our answers in the town that does
not want us. Perhaps we will find the end to all the
answers."

There was a continued silence. Blue shifted his weight
gently, seeking for more comfort in pushing back against
the support of the cantle. There was a deep tiredness that
spooked him, as if he would never know a good horse or a
bright day without paying deeply for the pleasure. Damn.
There could be no tiredness now. He owed the man riding
beside him his life, maybe more.

This was going to be real easy. Better than the shooting
gallery they set up in the canyon with those weanlings.
Bristol Adderson rubbed one hand deep into his thick hair
and found the right spot. Then he brought the hand down to
settle against the trigger guard on the new Remington. It
weren't only the Mexican government could get a hold of
one of these beauties.

It was just like Vace told him. Here came the mex, riding
a fancy stepping, high-headed horse. And, by God, it was
Bristol's day all right. Along with the mex came that wet-
eared kid, riding right beside the big honcho. Gave him two
birds for a target instead of only one.

Adderson grinned. He'd taken enough of that kid up
north. The boss telling him to leave the kid be, let him work
his own way with the broncs. A baby's way. Then the kid
would grin at him and those damnable greeny eyes would

invite a good punch. Bristol felt the familiar anger rise in him. He was sure going to like pulling the trigger.

He heard the roan move behind him. And he remembered Vace's words. "You shoot that damned mex right off. He'll be coming right at town and riding with some 'a his men. You get him first and then the others." But Vace didn't know that the wet-nosed kid would be the one riding with the mex. Vace was a smart one all right, knew the gut shooting of the colts would bring the mex in on a hot temper. Didn't plan on the kid, though.

The sore-footed roan shifted nervously, raised his head and fluttered a whinny deep in his throat. Bristol sighted on the whiteness of the fancy shirt and squeezed. It was a pretty sight to see the blood spread across the shirt front, to watch the body lean back and drop hard, disappearing in the confusion of milling horses and rising dust.

He moved the sight of the big gun to look for the kid. He fired this time without taking aim and the bullet went wide and low, taking a chunk out of the light bay's hide. He watched the bay spin high and wild in a buck that sent the kid flying. Bristol laughed, then dropped back to his belly to take better aim.

The bay gelding had seen something ahead in the brush. Blue followed the horse's ears and saw the shape of another horse tied beyond a rock. His warning was lost in the boom of the rifle and he felt the shock as Rafael Maldinado spilled backward from the saddle. The buckskin jumped sideways and kicked at the body, while the bay spun in response to Blue's dig with the spurs. Blue lost his balance, and then the bay went out from under him in a tremendous buck. The shot blended in his ears with the horse's shrill scream.

Then he was lost in the tangle of dark legs and blurring sand. Blue rolled once and came up against the soaking red of the shirt. His hand reached out for the face of the downed man. There was no doubt, the shot had driven a fist-sized hole through the chest, exposing shattered bone and pink muscle. There was nothing Blue could do.

The bay was down, becoming a blockade from the sniper. The buckskin skittered into Blue, frantic from the blood smell, and kicked at Blue's reaching hand. Blue came up to grab at the horn, letting the horse's spin pull him into the saddle. He drove the horse over the thrashing bay in a straight-up leap that carried them closer to the sniper's rock.

A shadow of a man slid from the brush and mounted the untied horse. Blue dug in deeper with his spurs, then leaned down and pulled the sheathed rifle free. The reins hung loose from the long shanked bit and slapped the buckskin at each stride, driving the horse into a faster run. Ahead of them the roan took laboring strides to get away from the madman coming up fast.

Even running free the buckskin was the better horse, Blue the better rider. There was no chance for Bristol to get away. The heavy man knew that for a fact and took his only chance. He yanked the roan to a halt and half fell from the saddle. Reins still bunched in his fists, he raised the rifle and aimed at the wide chest of the fast-approaching buckskin. He waited one moment longer and his target came closer, until he could not miss. Close enough that the wild blue eyes brought back all the hatred, and made the shot a pleasure.

He knew this man. It was Bristol Adderson. Blue shot twice from the back of the buckskin, and missed. The buckskin was out of control now, running from panic into certain death. The braided reins swung at his shoulder, hitting him in each stride. He brought Blue straight at the kneeling man, and Blue could do nothing but keep pulling the trigger and wait for the killing shot.

Adderson raised his sights to center on the loose body leaning over the buckskin's shoulders. He lost his nerve and lowered the barrel, pulled the trigger, and watched the buckskin horse go down on his knees, plow into the sand with his nose, and flip over to land with his head buckled under the lifeless body.

The Henry flew high and came down barrel first to jam into the sand. The kid went wide and Bristol thought he had gone clear. Then one long leg kept its connection with the stirrup, jerking the kid back to stay with the falling corpse and lie still half-under the dead weight.

Bristol grabbed the sweaty roan and rode. He wasn't going to take any chances at all. He shoved spurs into the stumbling horse and lined out toward Tucson. He'd leave the rest of this one for Vace. The mex was dead, the kid down. That was enough for Bristol.

He crawled out from under the weight of the dead horse. Crawled because he could not stand. He knew that Rafael Maldinado was somewhere behind him, and began to retrace the last moments he could remember, quartering the tracks made by the wild running horse, fearful he would lose contact with his man. There were times when the effort was too much and he plowed into the sand to sleep. Then he could come to his hands and knees again and continue the search.

Annuncio saw it first. Something making a ragged line across the ground scattered with brush. Without turning his head, he spoke softly to Mickey, and the Indian put his horse to a lope. Annuncio had already seen the silhouette of a lone horse, standing on three legs, saddle empty. That was not good.

The hand on his shoulder pushed hard into Blue's mind, tried to stop his motion. He leaned into the pressure, butted his head against the leather stockinged legs, but his tormentor would not give way. His arms buckled and Blue fell, rutted sand scouring his chin.

Then that same implacable hand rolled him over, and

Blue looked up into the dark face of the Indian. Mickey. Blue began to understand. He sat up on his own, and looked for what should be there. His red-rimmed eyes flashed by the Indian, and the man grunted at the color, a blue clouded storm.

The old man was sitting on the high-stockinged sorrel. Blue could only point; he raised his arm and showed the old man and the Indian where he was. In the dry wash. Blue accepted the strong hand and came to his feet, staggered into the solid bulk of Mickey and steadied himself on wide shoulders. They watched the old man guide the sorrel down into the shallow dip. Mickey walked after him. Blue took a tentative step and found he could follow.

It was not easy to stand and look down at the stilled body. By turning his head, Blue could look back and see the outline of the bay gelding, ground tied by the steaming corpse of the buckskin. The bay must have wandered there to find comfort out of the pain. Mickey rode his gray back and picked up the reins of the bay. The crease across his rump had finished its bleeding and the horse would survive.

Annuncio talked in low murmurs to the Indian. Blue did not want to know. Then Mickey slipped from the flea-bitten gray and gave the reins to him, motioning for him to mount and slide back over the saddle. The body of the Señor was balanced carefully across that saddle, and Mickey mounted the lamed bay. They would take the Señor home to his wife, to his child. Then they would come back with the young man from the north, and they would find the man who had done this. His death would not be fast or pretty.

★ Chapter 10

Charles Evans Warner found it hard to look in the mirror sometimes. He knew too well what he would see: the newly-added lines, the sag to the wide jaw, the downward pull at the thin mouth. There were wrinkles and lines added daily. He took to letting his hair grow, and let his sideburns bush out to a wildness. There was only hatred in the face he saw in the mirror now.

And the only reason he was looking was the load of liquor he was carrying. The quart of trading whiskey had made the rounds as they waited at the small iron gate. Yesterday he had stood in the line as they buried Henry Wallem, and today they had buried Rafael Maldinado at the ranch. And today Charlie Warner had gotten stinking drunk.

He turned too fast, lost his balance, and caught himself on the thick plastered walls. Their feel gave him comfort; not for him and his Rosa the fancy dressing of the wood-framed house and horsehair plaster. Warner snorted and stood straighter in the gloom of the long hallway. Damn fool notion to live in double stories when the heat ate you alive most year 'round. Not for him.

'Course, that he couldn't pay for the luxury of such a

monster had no bearing on his disdain. Charlie snorted again and walked the distance from the clatter outside the front door to the quiet of the small courtyard.

A shame, to bury a man such as Rafael Maldinado with only his riders and his family in attendance. The man pulled his weight when this was a frontier town. Damned shame. The tall anglo had been to the funeral; Charlie had seen him standing behind the new widow and her child. Been riding with Rafael when he got shot. And word was spreading that the blond kid might have been the one to bring Maldinado down. Didn't sound likely to Charlie; he saw the trust the missus put in the presence of the boy. Not likely.

Shame came back over him in a wild loop, dropping his head and making Charlie Warner fight for his uneven balance. Rafael Maldinado had been his friend for almost eighteen years, since before he married the pretty lady from the train. And yet Charlie had let the talk and the fancies of new power sway him from his friendship, his obligations, and his pleasures with their family.

Charlie slapped his hand down on the dust-covered foldup top to the piano. Something his wife 'had to have,' some fool thing she never touched but to wave a hand at and brag some on him. He bought it for her, and went near to bankruptcy with her whims. While he let a friend go who was proven strong.

Ruth Maldinado had stood bareheaded by the mounded grave, sunlight picking up the gray in her fine auburn hair. The daughter, Celita, was beside her mother, showing the same strength in her set back and proud head. These were not people who had need of a piano or a flight of stairs and a yard of bleached grass.

The self-pity put him in the need of another drink. He was coming too close to thinking on right and wrong, coming too near the anger that rode him each day in the store. Another bottle would back up the feelings and cork

the thoughts. Let him open up the store in the morning and
be willing to wait on the few customers. Hell with it, he'd
take another drink and open up this afternoon.

"Ma'am. We riding out now. Just wanting to know you
be all right alone. This got to be settled now. We wait too
long and those tracks get covered over. Mickey, he and
Annuncio can follow what's left. Me, I'm going for the ride
and to find the big-bellied man did the shooting. Knowed
him from Utah. Just wanting to know you're all right for
now."

Ruth Maldinado knew what the boy was trying to say.
But the harsh, spoken words still hurt. She could see into
his face and read his mind. Yesterday, only yesterday,
Annuncio had ridden in with the gray horse on a line, the
body hanging across the saddle, the boy riding the rump of
the tired animal, hands steadying the corpse of her husband
in the saddle.

She had not cried. There had been no surprise for her,
only a pain deep inside that would not soften with time. Her
words had come as comfort to the old Annuncio and the
sullen-faced Mickey. The tall blond anglo had kept to his
silence long enough to put up the horses, then had fallen
into a sleep that brought him to this morning.

The simple burial in the small iron-rimmed piece of
ground freed the men. She asked only that they wait until he
was buried. Now they could ride and now she would return
to the few hours of her private grief. Celita had taken the
yellow mare and ridden into her hills. Soon mother and
daughter would come back to work the ranch and to live
with their pain.

She looked up at the boy. There had been no hesitation in
him, no holding back. "Why are you doing this? Why do
you ride out with Mickey and the old man? Your debt is
canceled and you are free. I have the bill of sale for a horse

of your choice, and your gold piece. You have never taken them. Rafael said to wait, that you would come to him. But you are staying to fight for a cause that is not yours. Why?"

She was asking more than he knew. Blue shifted his feet, pulled at a lock of hair sliding past his eye. He didn't have the words that would give her a good answer.

"Ma'am, the Señor. He give me a place, a trust. Don't know how to say it. Figure I got a debt to him that I got to pay." He lost his nerve and shuffled back out of the dark room. The room where he had spent those long months. It was her mourning room now. His voice was loud enough to be heard beyond the thickness of the walls.

"We're riding now, ma'am. Back in a few days."

There was no need for talk among the riders. Mickey led, his flea-bitten gray walking out with long strides. Annuncio covered his back, off to the left and checking for what Mickey might not see. Blue rode farther back and to the right. He checked the ground but did not expect much. It was the two men riding ahead who would find the sign. Blue was the eye in the back of their heads.

The shallow wash and the body of the buckskin were easy; the indentations by the rock that gave the weight and size of the killer were there for anyone to read. It was the wild run back to the limits of the city that was the trouble. Not the trail, for even a day later it was clear, the hoofprints deep and wide-spaced in their speed, straight-lined to the streets of the city. It was the city that would give them the trouble.

Annuncio brought his high-stockinged sorrel up to the red bay of the boy. He knew Mickey's mind and knew that the Indian would not speak his thoughts. It was for him to ask the question. And for the light-haired anglo boy to know the answers.

"You know this man. He is the rider of the roan and the killer. Yet you say he is not the one to blame, that there is someone behind him. We cannot ride into the city and point our gun at his fat face.''

·''Señor Maldinado gave me a name as we rode yesterday. Vace Yarborough. Said he'd been riding lately with a fat man, fitted Adderson's type 'a friend. We find them in town, do some checking on their horses, whether they been around. Someone'll know something.''

The silence that followed set an edge to Blue, but he waited it out. Annuncio took his time thinking over the few words, then looked up at Blue and nodded as if something had been decided. Then the old man pulled back to put his horse alongside Mickey's gray. Blue waited, until Annuncio flicked his hand at him as if to move on a reluctant horse or a neighbor's dog. Guess he wanted Blue to get going. Guess it was left to Blue to make the entrance into town.

There was a swelling in his throat, a high lump that wanted to gag him. There wasn't enough to him to lead good men like these, to have them willing to follow his lead. He wanted to rein his pony a step back to fit in between the two riders. One look at Annuncio told him it couldn't be done. He put the bay to a lope and shortened the distance to town considerably.

He'd never been this far before. Been to a couple of wide-open cow towns up north, been once on the train to Chicago. Rode the box car with two fancy saddle broncs heading to a new city home. He'd been paid well for babysitting them, and lost it in one night with a pretty girl and a fast-talking bottle of whiskey. But he'd never been to Tucson before.

Blue put the wonder aside. He needed to find Yarborough and the fat man that rode with him. The rest of it: the odd angled streets, the wet greenery of the park at the end of the main road, the staggered two-story houses built between the street level adobe buildings of the old town, and the people

Lord, the people. He had to put all that away until there was time.

His head got stiff going from side to side, checking all the people flowing past him, headed in some other direction. Each time he turned, he could see Annuncio to his left, hunched deeper in the split saddle, hand resting protectively on his old rifle. Mickey came into sight from the right, dark face pulled pale, eyes never still, rifle out in the open and crossed over the saddle. One hand was clenched on the handle of a knife.

The words came out of nowhere.

"There's the man. There's the son of a bitch shot Maldinado. With the Indian and the old mex. He's a killer."

Blue hauled on the bay. Mickey's gray jammed into the horse's rump. Annuncio angled the sorrel to stand close and reached for his rifle. It was a short, gray-haired man, belly pushing at his leather vest, mouth wide, words coming out fast and ugly.

"I saw that son of a bitch. Waiting to shoot his own boss. Bet he and the Indian got fancy ideas. Got to keep this town safe. Can't have no killer like that 'un loose here."

Vace Yarborough thought fast. Never would have guessed the kid would ride right into Tucson looking for him. There he was, by God, sitting on a fine bay gelding, riding like he owned the town, with his escort crowding behind him. An Indian, too. Got him.

Geronimo running wild, Crook, Crawford and their men taking chase and finding only ghosts in the empty wind. Word kept coming back about meetings that never took place, talks that turned to dust. The Indian was his key. Vace's tone rose to a high pitch.

"Got hisself a chief for a bodyguard. That's the man, he done in Maldinado."

There were no calm minds to take a stand, to ask the right question. No law to wonder how Vace knew. The high scream of the words brought out a fever in those on the wide street. The three riders became a fearsome group, horses bunched and frantic, riders clothed in buckskin leggings and wide red headbands, rifles clear of the scabbards, held loose and ready to fire into the crowd.

Vace screamed again. Working on the noontime stragglers waking from a whiskey sleep. "Killed a man just outside a town. Killed his own boss, helped by the mex and that damned Indian."

Annuncio never heard the shot that entered his head, tearing out his brain and his life. The old man's body dropped from the comfort of the padded saddle and rolled in the dust under the wild, spinning horses. Vace grabbed a pistol from a man, took aim and shot in haste at the hatless blond head of his enemy. The bullet went past Blue's ear, taking the top off in a stinging scream. The crowd panicked at the explosion of shots, and pushed at each other in a scramble to get away.

Vace didn't want the kid ending up in jail, didn't want the law to hear the contradictions that would come from the kid's mouth. He knew enough to kill Vace in this town. The pistol kicked back in his hand as Vace pulled the trigger without sighting. The erratic aim brought down a thin-faced man wearing the stained apron of a butcher. The man sat in the middle of the chaos and put both hands to his belly. His own blood overlapped the animal stains covering his chest. The feel of its wetness drew a high scream of terror from him.

Vace picked up the scream, howling his addition to the growing crowd. There was no way the kid and the Indian could get out of this now. He shot twice in rapid succession, howled again in pretend pain and gloated over the satisfying results.

Hands reached for the gray's bridle, fingers tore the rifle from Mickey's grasp. It dropped free beneath the horse's front feet, kicked hard enough to splinter the stock and then was jammed under the steps. The bay gelding reared high above the crowd, forelegs dangling over upturned heads. The mass moved back from the menace of the shod hooves, and the hands dropped away from Mickey. Blue balanced the horse and held him in the wavering rear.

Blue spun the bay with his knees, left hand sweeping out to scoop up Mickey in the wide turn. The Indian scrambled onto the bay's rump as the horse came down hard. Directly ahead was the low entrance into a store. Behind them on three sides were angry people, searching for weapons, pulling out six-guns and finding the trigger guard. Blue dug in the spurs.

The horse slipped on the dust-scoured bareness of the wooden flooring. Charlie Warner heard the clatter of shod hooves on his downstairs planking. He put down the bottle hard enough to raise dust. The yelling and the shots were nothing new, but this intrusion was an outrage. He came halfway down the stairs, and saw the looming shape of a horse spin past the counter, knocking nails and the new shipment of hinges in a wild splurge of destruction.

He recognized the long blond hair of the rider. And knew the Indian perched half-off the bay's hind end. The bay came to a halt inches from his head; he shrank back, protected by the thickness of the railing. The rider looked hard at Charlie Warner and he knew an instant fear at the wildness in the odd blue green eyes. The horse settled, the Indian pulled himself snug to the cantle. And the rider kept his eyes on Charlie, making no move toward the revolver in its holster, shaking his head when the Indian touched a hand to the sheathed knife.

"No, he's got to give this to us."

Crowds were at the front door, jammed into each other at the width of the door, reluctant to make the first move into the dimness of the interior. Eager for their quarry. There was only a moment's time.

Charlie put both hands to the railing and slid his body underneath. Still holding to the rough wood, he dangled his legs and let go, landing almost on the chest of the bay. The horse only shuddered and raised his head, beyond anything that could spook him now.

"Quick. Follow me. There's a platform out here, and a road."

Charlie pushed past the horse and found the locked door, slipped the inside bolt and opened it, then ran the length of the stockroom to the double width of the loading door. He could hear the hesitation in the bay's steps as the blond-haired rider pushed through the narrow opening into the confusion of the stacked goods. It took Charlie another moment to slide back the two bolts of the big doors and open them to the startling brightness of the day outside.

The bay hesitated. Blue patted the sweated neck, and then drove in the spurs to push the horse onto the narrow edge of the platform. Mickey yelled, an eerie whoop that gave the bay the needed courage, and the big horse jumped out from the platform, shod hind feet sliding on the slick wood, knees buckling as the weight of the two riders slipped forward on the landing.

They were free. Behind him Blue could hear the voices rise, boot heels hitting the planking, words yelled in outrage. Mickey slapped the bay hard with the flat handle of his knife, while Blue dug in the spurs remorselessly. The horse came up from the dust and bucked into the narrow street, headed north in a hurry. Headed through the proper homes and watered lawns to the safety of the mountains. Blue yelled with each stride, Mickey bounced and flailed at the panicked horse with his legs. They were free.

At the front of the small store, now jammed with the angry yelling of newly-brave men, Vace Yarborough turned to his fat companion. There was a shine to Adderson's face, a sweated fear.

"Bristol, we got trouble. You better find that kid and the Indian, make your shots count this time. You got yourself into a mess this time. And there ain't much I can do about it."

Vace grinned at the confusion in Adderson's round face. The mex was dead, the kid on the run with the question of a killing over him. And Bristol Adderson on his trail. The law in Tucson would not bother with the riders hightailing it for the hills, and the county law was taken up with the Indian ruckus. What was one more long rider with a dead mex to his name? Vace liked the odds: the old man dead, the kid and the Indian on the run, and the ranch back up in the mountains run only by women now. It would be the making of him yet.

★ Chapter 11

There was a light at the house. Blue shivered and huddled deeper into the canvas jumper. He thought this was the desert; not right to be shaking cold at night and steaming sweat in the day. He let the bay come back to a slow walk. Mickey waited behind him in the back of a slanted boulder, to watch their back trail and listen for pursuit. Blue needed only a minute at the ranch to ask a few questions and pick up gear and a mount for Mickey.

Tucson. The city lights were dim and far off to his right, but in the clarity of the desert air they could be counted from this high in the mountains. He still did not understand what had happened in the town two days past. He knew that Annuncio was dead and he and the Indian had escaped; that men had followed them until they reached the confines of a high-walled canyon at the base of the northern mountain range.

Mickey knew the trails. It was he who guided Blue and the bay by short grunts and hand signals. They had stopped once, to set up an ambush that brought down none of the riders but took three horses out. It was enough for the quick-tempered posse to retreat with double-loaded horses. The

dark cut off the posse from their quarry, and retreat was the
only solution.

Away from the angry crowd, the wild yells of hatred,
Blue put his trust in the silent Indian and followed the
winding maze. It brought them across the slopes to the
west. They stayed below the height of the ridge, winding
slowly between the fallen rocks, watching the cactus claw
and thorny bush. Two days working their way in the early
light, then holing up until daylight faded. Two hungry days.

Blue suspected that the law would be waiting at the
Single M. He came down to the back side of the ranch, to
the spring pens used only for branding. There were two
horses picking over the remains of a hay pile. The tired bay
sighed with the release of the cinch and the rush of cool air
across his hot back. Blue roped the big dun and Maldinado's
favored brown. His hands trembled as he rigged the saddle
in place. He could feel his whole body begin to shake.

A pebble rattled against another. Blue spun on his heel
and went into a crouch, hand carrying the revolver that
came up without thought. Then he rose unsteadily, feeling a
red flush come up his neck and along his face. Thank the
Lord for the near darkness.

"Blue, what happened? We've heard so many stories."

Her voice was sweet to him, the slenderness of her
something he wanted to draw with the tips of his fingers.

"I can bring you supplies, a coat, some food. You and
Mickey need more than just horses." She stopped and the
words came with a struggle. "We know about Annuncio.
Mama would not let us open the coffin. He is buried up with
Papa."

Then the anger came back. "They were here looking for
you. And blaming you for Papa's death. Mama was very
gracious and said we would send word."

There was a long hesitation in the talking. Blue huddled
into himself and waited for the condemnation.

"Here." Celita held up a saddlebag, each side thick with necessities. "I have had this ready and waiting for you to come get the fresh horses. There is a saddle and gear for Mickey on the fence."

How could he have doubted her? She knew him well, cared for him through the fever days. Blue smiled at his own stupidity as he gently lifted the leather bag from her hand.

It was a relief to have him standing in front of her. Celita looked hard at the young anglo with the blond hair growing wild and long, the blaze in the blue-green eyes cautioned by the hard days. The paleness had gone, the insolence tempered by reality.

Following the days of worry and the nights of wonder, Celita took the three steps that separated her from Blue. She leaned into his body, head reaching under his chin. There were no words from him, no groping hands or rough kisses. It was enough to stand there, pressed lightly against him, hearing the steadiness of his heart, knowing again the strength in his body.

Blue was afraid to breathe, afraid that the thudding of his lungs and heart would spook her. It was a sweetness he had never known, a trust that was not part of his life. The grass-fresh smell of her hair, the soft curve that fitted into his hips and leaned against his thighs.

He did not need to be told; he leaned down and put his mouth to the wire sharpness of her hair and pressed gently. She stirred softly and brought a wildness with her movement. Then she lifted her head and stood up on her toes. They touched at the mouth.

Blue backed away suddenly. Celita was alone, eyes following his retreat. "Blue, there is more you must know. Please wait."

Instinct told him to run; desire and shame kept him turned

away. She was a child still, not yet a grown woman. He could not look at her.

"There's a warrant out for you and Mickey. They say you killed Papa, and they have a witness. There are men waiting everywhere for you. There is a reward out and the law wants you back in Tucson anyway it can get you there. Be careful."

These were sobering facts. Blue came around to look at the girl, to listen to her story.

"They let us have Annuncio, but they promise to hang you, and to butcher Mickey. Everyone is frightened about the Indians. They've left the San Carlo reservation again. It is only Mama and I up here now, and the few vaqueros who do not have families. The rest have gone back to their homes and their families. The whole valley is afraid."

"Miss, get the men to return here, to the ranch, and bring their families. The gardens can grow again next year. Your pa built a fortress up here and you all will be safer. You'll have your own army."

What he said was of great practicality, but why did he find it so easy to walk away from her, to talk of ordinary matters? Why did he not watch her face, or touch her hair? Celita twisted her fingers together, willing them not to reach up and slide along the ridge of bone just below his eyes, or touch the silkiness of the matted yellow hair. The echo in her mind was of his heart, not her own. How could he stand there and not hear the sound?

Blue saw the change in her eyes, felt the warmth in his belly. He needed out of here, quick.

"Thank you, Miss. Obliged for the supplies, and the horses. Be on my way." He choked, spat, and tried again. The words were muted and not enough. "I thank you."

It wasn't what she wanted. The supplies and the horses. Over the quiet steps of the two animals, she spoke her own thoughts.

"I love you, Blue Mitchell. I love you."

The words were the right ones and she was glad they were spoken, even if only to the wind and the hard-packed ground. She did not know that Blue Mitchell had stopped walking at her voice and heard what she said. Words he had never heard before.

He rode blindly into a hand that pulled the red dun to a stop. It was the Indian who looked up at him from the blackness of the shadowing boulder and grunted at his gringo slowness. Blue's head swiveled at the sound, and saw the dark face. Mickey.

He tugged and brought up the saddled brown, wordlessly handed the reins to the Indian who was in the saddle from the off side. For one moment longer they sat in the dark, able to count the clear new stars. There was a fresh eagerness to the two horses, a drive in them to move on.

Mickey pushed two blunt-tipped fingers into Blue's arm and brought his hand to his mouth, circling his open lips to mimic eating. A smile crossed Blue's face at the gesture. As they rode they poked into the stuffed bags to find hard biscuits, beef jerky, salt bacon, and coffee grounds. On top there was a treat: a tin of cooled stew, sweet with wild onion and carrot greens. Blue used his finges to shovel the thick liquid into his mouth, and watched as Mickey worked his own meal with quick hands. There was a grin in the dark eyes, a smile blurred by the eating motions. Blue nodded. Nothing had ever tasted better to him, either.

With no words, there was a transfer beween the men. Mickey took the brown off the narrow path and set the horse to climbing up the impossibility of jumbled rock and cactus. Blue followed; it was Mickey's show now. The horses scrambled around the bigger rocks, stopped to scent the thin trail, settled on their hocks, and picked front legs over sharp ledges, dropping down carefully to new ground.

The food settled into an urge to sleep. The edge sharpened by two days of running was wiped out by their full bellies. Blue's head nodded as he dropped into moments of sleep only to be brought awake by a jump from the dun horse, then lulled back into sleep by a few strides on level trail. Mickey knew where they were headed, even in the darkness.

Blue jerked awake from a hand reaching for his elbow. He looked into the grinning face of the Indian and felt the heat color his face. They were standing in a small piece of flat ground, sheltered from invading eyes by overhanging rock. Mickey slid from the brown, knelt to the ground with the reins tied to his wrist, and lay down with closed eyes.

Blue followed Mickey's lead, but took time to look where they were. There was only room for the two horses. No graze, no water, no sweet brush for the horses to chew. Only hard ground hidden by leaning walls. A safe place for a good sleep. As he stretched out on the comfort of the rocky floor, Blue watched the stars blacken out, obscured by the tip of the rock ledge. He thought to work on what to do next, and was asleep before the thoughts came together.

Where would those two go with the whole valley after them? Celita stayed too long at the back corral, watching the spot where Blue had disappeared leading the extra horse. She mourned for her father, grieved with her mother, and wanted to ride with the man who was supposed to be the killer.

She walked easily in the blackness, knowing the ground under he feet well enough to move blindfolded. She would stay with Mama for now, and they would call in the vaqueros and their families to make up a private army. The blue jacket army was on the move against the Indians, and revenge would be taken. There were already stories of silent raids and murdered clans.

She almost let her thoughts go back to the tall anglo riding the mountains tonight, but forced her mind to stay with the immediate troubles that she could deal with. It would have to be her faith that stayed with him, not her thoughts, or her body.

There was little of comfort through the short days of winter. Mickey kept them moving constantly, finding hideaways deep in the mountains, coming out to find better graze or to search for game. Blue followed the Indian blindly, and grew used to the sight of the square-shouldered back and banded black hair. He accepted the leadership without question.

It was existence now. Running from constant threat, hiding from any sign that did not fit in their narrow world. There were a few times they crossed the almost-hidden track of a long trail. Mickey would check back to Blue and point out the thin ribbon that followed to where the mountains smoothed out into the flatlands.

Blue had no interest in whatever importance this trail had for Mickey. He urged his dun across the faint track and back up into the safety of the mountains. He did not wait for the Indian to catch up.

★ Chapter 12

There was a change in the air. The days were longer, colder, with periods of rain that battered their bodies, soaked into the horsehair padding under the saddles, split the threading on boots and clothing. Blue shivered in the wet and rode in constant misery. The rain seemed to run off Mickey's shoulders and down the outside of his hightopped moccasins.

A fire took forever to light. Mickey chose a good site, under a slab of rock, but the water-soaked wood did not burn. Mickey watched the young man who rode with him, and felt a worry build in him. Face drawn, shoulders high, shaking with the bitter wetness, the boy moved head down and silent. A dry cough started, and there was a flush of red high on each cheek.

There would have been lung damage in the bullet that had almost taken the young one's life. And the narrow-brimmed hat, the threadbare shirt, and worn canvas jumper did not offer the needed protection. Without fire, food, and warm clothing, this one would sicken again and die. It was for Mickey to plan so that did not happen. It was for the young señorita that the gringo must live.

The fire caught this time, the warmth feeble in the damp of the night. Mickey risked broadcasting their camp and roasted a small hare he trapped. The meat was good, hot and greasy. Not enough to put flesh back on the young one, but enough to warm the soul and almost fill the belly.

He boiled the bones and the innards in a small airtight and forced Blue to gag down the fat-soaked liquor. It would be enough for this night, but there must be more, and greater, warmth. They would have to risk a return to the ranch.

Routine had been distilled to bare existence. Blue mimicked the Indian's daily chores, pulled grasses for the dun and the brown, made snares from braided horsehair thongs, saddled and rode behind the brown gelding, and dismounted and held the horses while Mickey disappeared. It was a passive series of days with no need or desire between the two men to speak.

This morning was no different, except that Mickey watched the gringo with speculating eyes, counting the slowness of his work around the horses, the stiffness as he packed and tied his gear to the saddle, picked clean the bones of the camp, and stood to mount. It took him three tries to get his boot in the stirrup. And there was the coughing, more frequent, with a ragged dryness that would double the boy with its draining power.

Blue paid no mind to where the horses put their feet, where Mickey would choose to ride. He had come to a smallness in his days, where it was his work to draw air in and push it out from his lungs, where the heat in his body warred with the coolness of the winter air, then turned on him to bring a chill that shook him in the saddle. The dun knew to walk in the brown gelding's footsteps, and there was no need for Blue to put a hand to the knotted reins.

This day the dun walked quietly, sometimes slowing when his rider bent double to one side of the horn, shiftin weight to threaten the dun's footing. So it was the brown who first sensed the difference, who quickened his step in anticipation. This was home range. The brown horse jigged, tossing his head and ignoring Mickey's slap on the side of the neck. This was home range.

Blue lurched forward in the saddle and almost slid off as the big dun horse gave a half buck. Mickey's raised hand brought both horses to a halt. Blue leaned over and gagged at the constriction in his chest, the bitterness rising into his mouth. He spat and looked away from the bloody mixture that slid off the shiny circle of the flat-sided cactus.

The horses stood sprawling downhill, front legs propped on a tumble of rock washed free by the winter rains, hindquarters uphill. Beyond the bottom of the wash and behind a small plateau was the Single M hacienda, the home ranch. Mickey's head turned side to side. There was a single gunshot, softened by the drone of the rain. The shot was doubled, then the sounds blossomed into a constant volley.

Mickey lifted the brown into a sliding run. He did not look back; he knew that Blue would follow the sounds, hugging himself to the big dun, riding for the life of those at the ranch. They hit the flat ground at a gallop. The brown put his head down and squealed with the pleasure, letting out a wild buck that Mickey took with a sliding grace. Blue dug in spurs to the dun; one buck and he would be gone. The horse put his nose out and ran.

Even above the wind at their ears and the staccato firing, they could hear the wild cries. They did not need the sound to know: Indians. Raiding the ranch and finding two women. There was a difference in the sounds, a deepness to the boom of the Sharps, a hollow lightness to the quick action of the Winchesters.

Mickey pulled to a sliding stop; the dun slammed into the brown in his own effort. The Indian was off with rifle in hand and on one knee before Blue slipped his feet from the stirrups and came down the off side of the dun. He brought the Henry with him, steadied the sight with his elbow on a bent knee, and found himself a target in the back. He sighted high up, between the shoulder blades. He had to blink rapidly to keep the moisture from his eyes.

Then Mickey pulled the trigger, Blue only a beat behind him. They were close enough to see the blood jump from the widening hole in the target's back. Blue coughed twice and spat, then fired again. The Indians were up and gone from the new attack, quick to find their tied horses and spread down the hillside in staggered retreat. These were not odds to their liking.

Blue quit firing first, eyes blurring from the rain. He bent double and dropped the Henry into the new red mud. The coughing blocked out the silence of the rifles for him, and the cheering from the house. He only knew the fury in his chest, and the bitterness that wanted to choke him down.

It was Mickey that lifted him to stand, turned him to the dun and hoisted him partway to the stirrups. He picked up the reins from both horses and started down to the ranch. Blue wrapped his hands around the horn and rode against the sway of the walk. It was all he could do.

"Mickey. And Blue. You've come back to us."

It was a sweet sound. Blue's head came up, his hands relaxed their grip on the horn. Mickey stopped his walk and pushed the single rein into Blue's fist. The gesture brought a smile to Blue that turned into a deepening cough.

"Get down, come in the house, and get warm. We will take care of the horses. Come in, there is so much to talk of." That was a different voice, carrying a reserved warmth that Blue could understand. He nodded down at the familiar face of the Señora Maldinado and accepted her invitation.

They came into the house to a welcoming of men and women, small children in long-tailed shirts, and infants sti' crying from the harshness of the short-lived battle. Celita was waiting for Blue, to put a woolen blanket around his shoulders and tuck the ends under his arms, wrapping him in the welcomed warmth.

Blue kept walking, knowing what she was doing but with no strength left to smile and thank her. His steps carried him in the familiar pattern, under the low lintel of the big room door and to the right to the short passage that brought him against the half door of the small room. There were children playing in there, on the floor, tears staining their baby-soft faces.

They did not matter; he fumbled at the latch and accepted her help. The bed was there, covered with a green striped blanket and a multitude of straw dolls. She reached the bed before him and wiped the blanket clean. Blue dropped his shoulder and leaned in a roll that eased him on the bed, found the softness of the feather stuffed pillow, and instantly was asleep.

Celita pulled the blanket over his feet, not caring about the red mud that would crack and dry, that would stain the fine woolen blanket and white muslin sheets. She smiled down at the sleeping man, and leaned to kiss him.

A child giggled behind her hands, and whispered to her companion. The room burst into laughter as Celita herded the children out. She enjoyed their pleasure, for it matched her own. She followed the children in to hear the voices of the grownups as they talked.

"Mickey, they came about forty minutes ago. We think there were ten. They were not with Geronimo, but were led by Ulzana. Julio has seen him before. This is our first time for such a raid. We are thankful that the families came here to live, and that you and Blue were enough to drive them off.

"But what about you being here? It still is not safe. He is wanted for my husband's death. And you also. They will not listen to me, they will not accept my word that he is one of us, and that you are our family. They will not come here in the rain, but when it ends you must ride on. We will put together supplies for you. But for tonight, we will have our own fiesta."

The room was cleared after the long meal was finished. Estaban brought out the guitar, Julio found a fiddle of the Señor's, and they put their music together. Even the children danced, hugging each other in their excitement, enjoying this as if it were Christmas again.

Mickey danced, whirling like a madman with a round and smiling woman named Esperanza. Ruth Maldinado sat alone, hands clapping with the rhythm, eyes sparkling with the tears she could not show. She did not look for her daughter; no one did. They all knew the Señorita would be gone for the night. Sitting at the bedside of the blond-haired gringo child.

Two days. He slept two days. All he remembered were gunshots and mud. And the endless rain. The soft brush of Celita's hair as she leaned over to touch his face. That was the best memory.

It was Mickey who brought the outside world back to Blue. He came in the small room carrying a canvas warbag, top open and half-full. He set it down hard, pushed it with his foot toward Blue, and grinned a wild, split-tooth grin. A quick circle of his hands let Blue know they were to ride out this evening, that they would use the darkness to cover their leaving. He had forgotten the existence of the outside world, and for a moment hated Mickey for reminding him.

He would not look at the odd green bag. If he did, then he would have to accept leaving. Instead, Blue stretched out on the comforting sag of the bed. This was the first place he ever belonged, and now a damned Indian was makin certain he left. God, he hated Mickey. Blue closed his eyes against the craziness of his thoughts and went back to sleep.

Something gentle brought him back. A hand stroking his chest, a line of warmth stretching from his shoulder to just above his ankle, the give and take of a bit of soft air on the outside fold of his ear. Blue knew better than to open his eyes. The gentleness might leave him stranded and alone again.

He rolled halfway in the bed, pulling his left arm above his head to make room for the mass of black hair, the face full of invisible freckles. His body shied away from the roundness of the flesh pressing into his chest, the wide heat touching at his waist. Then instinct picked up his free hand and let it drift from the tangle of the wire hair, along the pointed hardness of the shoulder, to the dropped curve that ended in an abrupt rise of soft flesh.

God, she was beautiful. And trusting. Blue had had a woman, a hard, brass colored woman, who had drawn him into her and stayed flaccid under his thrusts. She and the whiskey had taken his boyhood and his first money.

Celita was different, special, and willing to place herself up against him, take him as he wanted. Blue nuzzled into the darkness of the black hair and touched her forehead with his lips. A quiet sigh came from one of them, or both. He felt the softness of her eyelids with his mouth, the salty taste of her tears, the short strokes of hair that guarded her eyes.

His hand came up from her hip to follow the firmness of her back and hold to the boniness of her shoulder and pull her closer. Closer than he believed anyone could get.

They were gone by nightfall. Blue did not look back and Mickey did not wait. There was only the shadow of the Señora Maldinado to watch them as they rode back into the mountains.

It took a time of endless riding, of following Mickey's

back deeper into the hills. Blue shrugged into the warmth of the slicker and blinded himself to the world. Mickey did not push; he rode the brown and found hidden campsites. Rabbits were plentiful, and the dried beans and jerky packed in the warbag would feed them a long time. He could wait for the anglo to make up his mind.

"Goddamnit. I ain't sitting here no longer. This is a fool's way, Mickey. A damn fool's way."

Two heads came up, strings of grass hanging from slack lips. There had been no words spoken for a long time. Mickey did not turn his head. He had known for several days that there would be an explosion coming, and smiled at the growing volley of the sound.

"The Señor knew the man, name of Vace Yarborough. That's the son of a bitch put the law on us and did all the yelling. Comes to me, I ride into town, we do some working on my hair, darken me some, put a hat on and some different clothes and maybe I can get in. Alone."

Mickey's grin widened; the young gringo continued: "Ain't got much of a plan. But I got to do something. Got to find out. Think we can get me looking like somebody else? And you quit that god-awful grinning. We got to get me into that town."

Mickey looked at the anglo, noted what the months had done. A layering of muscle over bone, hands quick and confident, movements no longer awkward but of one piece. The face had grown and settled into its promise. The eyes no longer held the angry look of trouble, but carried a calm and steady promise. It was this one's time.

"Good. We start." Blue's head came up at the deep sound to the words. Mickey grinned, and held out his hand.

★ Chapter 13

The bottle slammed down hard on the long counter, and brought a foul oath from Vace Yarborough. Other heads turned, other hands went to unfamiliar guns strapped to shiny pant legs. Bristol Adderson paid no attention; he wanted another bottle, and damned fast. His last coin, a silver dollar, hit the bar top and spun in a short circle. Before it fell, the barkeep slid it into his apron pocket and put down the whiskey glass.

Vace wiped his hand across his mouth and then on his pants. Folks were sure nervous enough in this town. Word just come in that Captain Crawford's body been gotten out of Mexico, and them Indians had run off after making promises of peace with Crook. Enough to make anyone a jumping idiot. Even had trains ready to take the worst of the lot back east. Almost seventy-five of them savages. Good plan, but it failed, and had the local boys jumping at a rabbit's sneeze.

Word had gotten out; the 'Ring' was getting smug, didn't want the peace that would take the army away. Some talked about their sending a whiskey drummer down to spook the Indians with his talk. While some folks lost their homes and their lives, others brought in dollars from the army contracts.

Well, Vace hadn't got his dollar share yet. He'd been up with a few of the men supposed to be in this Ring, and got nowheres. Old Ernst Steinkellner was talked to be in this, with his fancy store full of pricey goods. But the ugly little bastard had only given Vace a few words of nasty-sounding English. Sounded more like a mouthful of dirty socks. The old bugger had called him crazy and turned him out of his establishment. But Vace, he was too smart to give up that easy. Word was out about him now, and he knew the 'Ring' was waiting for him to find the right man to step up to. The first move was his to make.

He elbowed Adderson in the ribs, and the heavy man swallowed his liquor and choked down a cough. The blank face swung around, anger sharpening the fuzzy edges. Vace never gave him a chance.

"You finish up there, Bristol, and give me a drink of that. We got to find the quartermaster supplying the troops. Out to the Fort. He's the son who knows. By God, I be getting old not to think on this before."

Vace shoved Adderson's reaching hand aside and brought the smudged glass to his mouth to drink down the remains of the whiskey, tasting the bitter sharpness to the reservation liquor. By God, he was right this time. Hit out to the south where them soldier boys was trailing, and talk to the supplier. So damned simple.

He left the big dun horse with Mickey. Too obvious an animal for him to keep, too easy a brand to read and remember. Blue knew he stood above the average man down here, but he and Mickey had done some practical magic up in the hills. Root dye darkened his hair, which they hacked short and covered with a wide hat; little d̦ was needed for his face and hands, stained by the new sun of the spring days.

But most of all, Blue no longer looked up. He walked with a proper humility that he put on with the loose shirt, pants, and high-laced moccasins. Mickey figured this one out. Blue had to learn to go small in his mind, head tilted, eyes cast down, staying deep inside, where he kept the child hidden. There was no place in the charade for anger or defiance. It was abject surrender for now.

Walking through the crowds would never come easy, but Blue found a freedom in no one looking at him. He could stand against a post and watch, his gaze sullen and withdrawn, his eyes hidden by the tilt of his hat, and no one saw him. He stood at the edge of a gathering crowd, pushing close to a column outside Charlie Warner's almost barren store, to read a printed bulletin.

One man emerged from the crowd and pulled down the paper. His voice came out strong over the listening men.

"Dated April 6, 1886: Crook relieved of command, General Nelson Miles to conduct further chase and capture of all renegade Indians. Crawford's body on its way back to Nebraska. Geronimo and his band in the Sonora hills. Seventy-five Indians to be shipped back east on special train."

The crowd cheered, more men wandered over to join the celebration. Now there would be a finish to the Indian troubles, and a peaceable man could go about his business without fear of his home or his scalp. The notice meant little to Blue, except for the safety it meant to Celita and her mother. He moved away slowly.

He made himself count the steps past Warner's store. There could be no purpose to his walk, no sense that he was going to a certain place. Blue felt all the eyes watching him, calculating his intentions and his value.

He made it past the doorway to the end of the street, and

stepped into an alley to lean up against the wall and find his breath. He checked the street behind him, then looked into the length of the alley. White handbills covered the opposite wall, well-framed against the tan of the new wood boards.

His eyes drifted past the startling white squares, then came back in a hurry. The first instinct was to push away from his support and hurry to check what he saw. Mickey's words stuck with him: "Move slow, easy. No hurry."

Blue crossed the narrow strip of alley. No one would know the racing inside him as he came closer to the wall and read his own name and description from the frayed reader. Here was the listing of the formal charges against him and the $50 reward. His life wasn't worth much to these merchants, nor his supposed killing of an old friend.

"Adderson, you damned fool. Drop that bottle and it's the last whiskey for a long time."

Blue wanted to drop and spin, find the revolver that wasn't at the tip of his fingers. He leaned into the wall, loosened the pain in his shoulders, dropped his head, and went for an imaginary itch at his ear. His arm angled across his face, but he could see the shadows as the two men lurched past him. They never looked at the tall greaser getting at the louse biting him.

Adderson stumbled at the corner near Margeson's Butcher Shop, closed due to the death of its owner. The sharp elbow that dug into his middle went deep, and made him lose the bottle neck. Yarborough's two hands were cupped and waiting for it before Bristol could complain.

Then they disappeared, to leave Blue shaking with a coupling of anger and fear. He walked slowly, stayed a good distance. These two were headed someplace tonight. He had no plan but to take Vace out of Tucson to where he and Mickey could get the truth from the man. Bristol Adderson was a complication.

Blue shook his head. Adderson be damned. He couldr

take two men alone. It was Adderson who did the killing but it was Yarborough who sat on the horse and did the smiling. Bristol pulled the trigger, but Vace Yarborough did the thinking. Adderson would have to wait for now. Blue would have his man.

He watched the two weave a crooked line to the far livery barn. Blue had nothing but a sheathed knife, and in the next few minutes he had to take Yarborough free of the drunken Adderson and the volatile town.

He walked closer, almost on tiptoes, hand clenched white around the handle of the knife that Mickey gave him. The stable door swung open. The riders were highlighted for a short time as their fresh horses circled, heads back against restraining hands. Blue could hear the fury in Yarborough's voice as the man struck out with one hand. The slap against Adderson's flesh spooked the range horses as they pushed their way into the street.

Now or never. Blue stumbled into the light chestnut that Vace rode. His lurch caught the horse at the point of shoulder, putting the animal far enough off to loosen the rider. Yarborough's face came around to peer at the crouched figure in front of his bronc.

"You stinking greaser. Get the hell out of my way."

Blue's arms came up to hide his back from the lash of the split end reins. His erratic movements set off the pale buckskin Adderson rode. The horse spun in fright, and Blue heard more cursing as he pushed into the chestnut again, almost unseating Yarborough. Vace's temper busted loose.

The man pulled up one boot from the wide stirrup and lifted the leg, angling toward the crouching man. He lifted high, then jammed the boot down, raking the roweled spur across the exposed back. A deep groan from the covered head was his reward, and Yarborough grinned. He whirled the chestnut around the cowering man, pulling the other leg free for sport. Adderson hauled in the fractious buckskin and watched, then slapped his horse forward, swinging his feet free from the stirrups. He liked the new game.

Blue waited. He took the next spurring with a deeper groan that did not have to be forced. The line of pain brought sparks from his eyes. Head twisted under his arm, he could see Adderson's raised foot, tarnished spur headed for his face.

It was simple to grab the foot and turn it, putting all the anger into the bucking move that sent Adderson over the off side of his horse. The buckskin panicked at the flopping body, and one shod hoof clipped Bristol's head. He landed in a stilled heap.

Yarborough saw the abrupt dismount and laughed. Then he came around to stare at the tall man who now held the buckskin. He started his threat, then choked on it. Something was wrong. The man was staring up at him, eyes clear and wide, head thrown back. A smile was growing on the dark face to show a line of white teeth. Vace gagged at his sudden knowledge.

"Son of a bitch, it can't be you."

It was that anglo kid greased up to be a mex. But what the hell was he doing in town? At the livery stable? In front of the horses? Long fingers wound into the cheekpiece of the chestnut's bridle, and Vace felt the horse being pulled closer.

It was something his liquored mind had to deal with. Standing there in the middle of the damned street as if the town weren't looking for him, as if there weren't posters carrying his picture stapled up all over the damned territory. Vace opened his mouth to cry out, and found a sharp bite touching between his ribs. His hands tightened on the reins, his boots touched the horse's tender sides. The chestnut felt the signals and stepped deeper into the tall man that held the bridle.

"You move that horse one inch and you'll be needi

new lungs. Blade's well sharpened, you won't even know it's gone in. Settle that horse.''

It took effort to move his spurs from the heaving sides, to make his hands ease their grip on the leathers. Vace could feel the lightest tickle as something warm ran down his ribs inside his shirt. The son of a bitch had drawn blood on him. He took to breathing shallow, let his feet hang loose, then wrapped the reins around the horn and put his hands down, one on each thigh. He wasn't going to do nothing to move this horse around.

Blue nodded his approval, and Vace took the risk of a long breath. Bad mistake. The knife bit in again, reminded him. He went back to breathing short sighs, and watched the tall man beside him. It was whatever this bastard wanted right now.

Careful not to lose the tension of the blade between the ribs, Blue edged the chestnut around, pushing into the horse's shoulder with his elbow, bumping the head with his hand on the long shank of the curb. He stopped the cautious circle. There was the scraping sound of footsteps coming behind him. He could hear a gasp as Vace inhaled a short breath.

It was someone who walked with erratic steps, someone who stopped and cleared his throat, taking too long before he asked his question. Yarborough got smart and spoke up first.

"S'all right, Willy. Bristol got hisself kicked, got drunk and fell down and his damned horse kicked him. This fellow here is going to pick the bastard up and rehorse him. Now get the hell out of here.''

Vace choked on the lightness in his voice, the scratching in his throat. The words came hollow and false. Blue tightened his grip on the bridle, dug the tip of the blade in deeper, almost to where the metal wanted to slide into the warm flesh on its own. Blue had to hold back on the handle.

Vace gasped and one hand came to his side, brushed lightly against Blue's knuckled fist. Then both men were frozen in their separate worlds. It was up to the drunk, who stood there wide-mouthed and spraddle-legged.

Willy Bodwell never did like Vace Yarborough. Drank too much of other folk's liquor, faded out when the buying came 'round to him. And Adderson, good place for him lying out flat in the dust with a horse shuffling around him. Maybe the horse would take another chunk out of the son and there'd be less of Adderson to cart off.

Willy Bodwell liked to mind his own business, and he went by the pale face of Vace Yarborough and the big mound of Bristol Adderson and never thought anything more about them.

Blue dropped to his knee and reached for the pistol half-out of Adderson's holster. He had the gun in hand and was back at Yarborough's side before the man found the stirrups and thought about his own handgun. The knife slipped back into its sheath, and Blue rolled easily in the saddle of the buckskin. One hand cradled the pistol, aimed it at Vace's widespread belly. He pushed the horse into the chestnut's flank, put the gun deep into Yarborough's ribs, and nudged both horses into a measured walk.

"You ride quiet now, keep your mouth shut, and I won't blow you apart."

He turned the chestnut with his toe stuck into the shoulder to force the horse down the short alley and beyond the north end of town. Finally, he allowed the horses to move up into a lope. He stayed one stride behind, crowding the chestnut, pushing Yarborough into a panic.

"That horse gets one more stride beyond me and a bullet'll find the spot between your shoulders nice and clean. You made me a murderer, now you can be killed. You want to live longer, you ride with me."

They made a wide loop, and halted briefly when th

horses snorted their concern at the stream crossing. Vace cursed and thought of the day when he and Bristol had been out here, hiding in the brush, waiting for Maldinado.

Blue let the horses stop midstream to drink, and Vace suffered the hollow circle of the gun barrel in the flaring puncture made by the knife. He winced at the pain, then quieted.

"Just my way of letting you know. Just getting started. I read you, Yarborough. See your face every time I close my eyes. This is only the beginning."

★ Chapter 14

They did some fast scrambling and high climbing. Vace waited a long time, then gave up and let the horse carry him. Out in these foothills you couldn't run a horse, and Mitchell rode too close behind him, not allowing him the chance to run out. Vace figured it best to ride this one out and count his chances later.

The ground leveled out, the trail narrowed almost to a point, and Vace let his eyes close, his back slump into the horse. He knew Mitchell would get no sleep, and his own dozing gave him the beginnings of an edge. His head nodded in time with the four-beat step, and Yarborough slept.

There were three of them. Black hair greased to a shine, pulled into wrapped tails that hung along each side of their faces. Store-bought shirts, leather leggings, worked moccasins. Three faces that carried an evil in them. Vace started out of his sleep and looked back at Blue Mitchell. A wide grin split the hated face, lit into the wild sea-blue eyes, and sent a shiver down Vace's spine. Then his captor threw the pistol with an easy twist and one Indian picked it out of the air.

"You mine now. You will tell of what you did to the Señor. And you will tell true. These are my brothers. They have come to help."

Blue stood at the head of the chestnut and watched the effect Mickey's words had on the prisoner. Face blanched white, eyes wide, then shut against the fear. Blue turned away. It was the only path to choose, but he did not have to like it.

They pulled Yarborough from the saddle, the three men handling him as if he were nothing but a feed sack. Shoulders bouncing on the ground, he was dragged beyond the small fire, and propped backside to a rock.

They had talked of this. Of the need to pry from the gray haired man his reasons and names, dates; something that would stand up to the law. They would find the words in him, then have him repeat them to a witness willing to listen and to sign. It could take days, or hours. Time meant nothing in the mountains.

Blue shut his eyes. One hour with no sounds to tear at him. He came awake at the first whimper. Vace Yarborough stood tied to a rock, arms pulled wide to embrace the hardness, legs wrapped at the ankles, jerked tight under the rock edges, and tied firmly to a stake. He stood naked, his body shaking in the cold before the sun. Fat jiggling at his belly, genitals shrunken and pulled up from the bitter air. The whimper came from him in a steady flow, as his head rolled from side to side across the roughness of the boulder

The Indians sat on their haunches in front of him, not looking up at him but talking to each other in a quick succession of words and hands. Each held a knife, cousin to the one still sheathed at Blue's side. While he watched, one Indian brought his knife up to poke gently at the flesh hanging above Vace's knee. The small cry gave him much pleasure, and he grinned at his brothers, moving the knife in a small circle into the loose flesh. A bead of blood appeared.

Another hand came up, holding its own knife, finding its own soft spot on the pale body. A new sound, a choking cry, greeted this touch of the knife. The hand dropped back before the knife tip left its bloody mark. There was a long silence. Blue rolled from his blanket and walked past the three, working at making no big deal about not looking at the prisoner. Yarborough choked over the name, then called out:

"Mitchell, you tell them to stop. I ain't . . . " Blue did not look at him, but sank to his heels and reached for the small pot bubbling over the banked fire. Hot coffee, the way to wake up and find the new day. Even without sunrise. He poured his cup full, put the pot back into the coals, and brought the steaming liquid to his face. A wonder. Both hands cupped for warmth, he tipped the coffee and took his first sip. Sighed, coughed against the releasing heat, and took another sip. He could feel the eyes watching him.

It was Mickey's turn. His jab was stronger, his aim higher, closer. He found a muscle and traced its narrow line of red along the inside of the thigh, following the slack line that went higher into the groin. Yarborough tried the impossible, to pull himself away from the sharpness of the knife, the line of its attack. He could feel the honed point prick at his testicles, and screamed.

Blue bit down hard on his lip, wrapped his fingers tighter around the tin cup. Anything not to let his anguish show. He felt the memory of the six gun in his hand meeting the swinging head, taking out the jellied mixture of the eye. His stomach turned over hard, and he choked on bile.

Then he walked carefully between Mickey and his brothers to stare in Yarborough's face. Blue took a big gulp of the cooling coffee, sighed in contentment, and swallowed. He waved the heat of the cup across Yarborough's face, not offering the teasing liquid, but letting the aroma heighten the rawness of the day and savagery of the three men who squatted below him, looking up at the hanging swell of his belly and the vulnerability of his manhood.

"They ain't done nothing to you yet, Vace. And won't do nothing if you speak up. Got to give us the right words and put them down on paper. Then we get them signed. Real simple. Just want to clear my name."

There was a time of silence. Blue looked past the camp to the beginning shine of the sun, picking its way up the side of the mountain. Lines of light caught the metals imbedded in the rocks, colors broke into the dullness of the gray sky.

"Going to be a pretty day, Vace. Enjoy it. Could be your last one. Take a good look."

Blue gave him no time but walked away, stopped to refill his cup, and found a soft spot next to a smooth-shaped rock. He nodded to Mickey, and the Indian brought his knife up, very slowly retracting the muscle up into the groin. The flesh puckered and twitched with its own life, and Vace howled. The Indian showed nothing as he found the tiny point of blood he had drawn before, and put the sharp tip to the same spot, going deeper this time, cutting through the hairy outer covering of the skin, touching the round shape inside.

The howl grew. Eyes wild, mouth open to an impossible size, the sound came from Vace in increasing waves. Tears flowed down his face and his head thrashed from side to side, hitting the rock with a soft and rhythmic thudding.

Blue let the sounds go over him. It was Maldinado and the girl. He pictured the blown-apart body sprawled in the dirt, he saw again the tears track down the brown, freckled face. Her soft words, the warmth to her eyes that brought a heat to him. Anything to block out the terror that came from the faceless white form lashed to the rock.

The scream came to form words that stopped the pain. "I'll tell you, I'll sign anything. It was Adderson shot Maldinado, Adderson put that rope over you. It was Adderson."

Mickey turned his knife twice in the clean sand and returned it to its sheath. He looked at the sagging white man. Stripes of blood ran slowly down his blue-veined leg, pooled at the fleshy pocket above the knee, then fell in tired drops to the ground. The man had lasted longer than Mickey had thought. Not long enough for Mickey's taste.

His brothers came to stand next to him. They spoke softly, and Mickey answered, keeping one eye on the tall and dark-haired man who had not yet moved. Then Ketah picked up the small bundle of his belongings and pulled out the yellow striped blouse that spoke of his rank. Joseph shrugged into his own version of the blouse, which lacked the constriction of sleeves.

They walked past the tall, young white man, brushing shoulders against him, taking his nod as their due. They mounted two horses, rode around the piling of rock that blocked off the small gully, and were gone.

It was Mickey who untied the ropes and released Vace Yarborough, but would not give the man his clothes. He did allow him a scant cup of the bitter coffee, then propelled the shivering man to stand where Blue was settled.

He did not look up, but handed Vace three sheets of paper and a thick stub of shaved pencil.

"You write it all down. Every word. And I'll see Mickey keeps to the other side of the fire. All of it, Vace. Every goddamn word."

It was hard for him to keep the anger from surfacing, hard to keep his hands off the puke-white face. What Mickey and his kin had done only captured Blue's anger and magnified it. He was shaken to find he had grown accustomed to the sounds and the screaming, and had relished the pain

Yarborough was feeling. It would never be enough to wipe out the pain he had caused.

Blue clamped down on his temper and shortened his words. He stood slowly, finally wanting to face his enemy. Vace Yarborough did not take the paper. His hands hung from limp arms, his body shook with the early chill, yet he was too broken to hug himself and shiver into warmth. Blue rolled up the paper and jabbed at the hairless chest. Vace's head came up to stare at Blue, then look aside. The hands were slower, but they finally took the paper and let it unroll in loose fingers.

Vace sat down hard and stared at the whiteness in his hands. He had no idea how to start and what must be said. Blue watched the continuing silence, then spoke.

"You put down how you ambushed me with Adderson. Why you was after me. I heard you talking about the mare and using her to warn Señor Maldinado. You put that down in writing." He waited and watched the laborious writing appear on the page.

"It was you killed the weanlings. Write that out, tell them why. Then go to work on leaving Adderson to kill the Señor. Get it all down. Even how you framed me in town, setting those folks on us and killing Annuncio. Bet you fired that shot. I want all of it, Vace."

It took a long time, but Yarborough wrote out each word, pausing to work over his thoughts, writing for his life. Blue looked once at Mickey and caught the downpull of his smile. It was a bitter victory, and unfinished. But they watched Vace write his confession, and there was a release of new hope in them both.

They wouldn't let him sleep. Blue tossed Vace his shirt and pants, and watched as the man dressed, saw him wince as he drew on the smelly long johns over his pinpricked leg and punctured groin. Mickey quickly broke camp as if he knew where they were going. Blue accepted his lead and worked alongside the reticent Indian.

"Ketah spoke to me of a small group of soldiers and where they are camped. We go to them, to their chief, and have him listen. They will sign this paper with honor. Ketah say we can trust these soldiers."

This was the next step in the slow return to justice. Blue nodded his relief. He even helped the limping Yarborough mount the chestnut gelding. He would ride behind the man, keep a gun loose in his hand. After getting the bit of paper witnessed, Blue had thought of how he would get it to the town law. Riding into the city of Tucson would open him to a bullet. Mickey would be scalped and hung before he got past the streambed. And Yarborough would be with friends.

This time the trail took them down the eastern side of the mountains into the river basin. Mickey let them stop to water the horses and splash the coolness of the river over their dirt-streaked faces. Blue took handfuls of bottom sand and scrubbed at his hair, dunking his head under the flowing water to remove the stain. He watched the lines of black dye weave into the current and disappear. He worked his head over twice, feeling the tingle that the sand left, then burrowed under the water again, coming up with a mouthful that he spat into the clear air. One shake of his head and the newly blond strands slapped into his eyes. He looked through them to see Mickey watching, arms on knees, butt resting on his heels. There was a bright grin on the dark face that Blue knew was mirrored by his own smile.

Yarborough thought he saw a chance and reached for the chestnut's bit. Two hands gripped him, digging deep into his shoulder muscle at the neck. The voice was Blue's; the grip belonged to the Indian.

"Not this time, Vace. You come along with us. Mount up."

It was a pleasure to walk the horses along the riverbank.

The bottom land was flat and rich, growing miles of pale green spring grass. To their right rose steep-etched cliffs; beyond the reach of the water, to the east, the land went back to its scrub hills of cactus and spiky grass. They followed the river's course and took their delight from the moist land, the greenness of the cottonwoods, the signs of small game.

After an easy hour, Mickey picked up the pace, alternating from a trot to a quick bursting run, then a breather and a few minutes of walk. The land changed, with subtle signs like thinning grass and small clumped plants. The horses strained to take the small hills at a trot; the riders braced themselves to come down into the washes. To their right, the mountains slowed their height, dipping down to become softer hills.

Blue wiped the pooled sweat from his neck, pulled his hat off and ran the bandanna across his forehead. They were moving south fast now. He watched Yarborough closely. There were several times when the man rode too loose in the saddle, almost tipping off from the ragged-gaited horse. Mickey never looked back. He would pull to a stop and cock his head, wait, then push his brown back into the long swing of the trot.

Mickey stopped and signaled Blue to come up beside him. As he pushed the dun past Yarborough, Blue tried to look into the man's face. Head down, face averted, the blue eyes refused contact, and Vace sagged into the swell of the saddle. Blue pulled the rein from his hand and dallied it around the narrow horn of this old hull. He had no trust in the man, beaten or not.

Mickey did not turn his head and Blue settled the dun beside him.

"There is a camp ahead. They are soldiers, three of them, and one chief. They do nothing but wait. I stay here, with him. You go."

It was a short walk to the camp. Blue kept to Mickey's direction and watched for a sign. The camp was not hidden. It was laid out in the center of an almost level bowl, hills swelling around it. It was not a war camp, not with the fire circle started and bedrolls stacked neatly against mesquite bush.

Three horses stood quietly at the picket line, tails going against the afternoon pests. Blue halted the dun as a man approached him. Hands folded in full sight across the horn, he watched the rifle muzzle. It rose gently and found its center on Blue's shirt, and was steadied by capable hands. Blue did not move. The dun cocked one hind foot and settled sideways.

The voice, when it came, was behind him. Blue set his teeth and clamped down on the impulse to spin and fight. This was not a war mission.

"What are you wanting with us, son? And why did you leave the other man behind with an Indian guard? Something we can do for you?"

★ Chapter 15

Blue pushed the dun horse around with his knee. The man with the rifle came with him, taking big steps to keep the barrel pointed at his target. The circle completed, Blue faced the speaker.

A man well into middle age, with some good height to him. A square face half-covered with a gray streaked bush of whiskers, eyes that looked right into Blue, and a strong body clad in a canvas jacket and pants. It was the hat that set Blue off, a flat circle of woven straw with a rounded top, shading the man's face but adding nothing to his dignity.

Blue grinned. The speaker's face opened into a slow smile that matched Blue's for pleasure. Then the third man, rifle still held easily, barrel ready to come up and fire square into Blue, came to stand behind the older man's shoulder. This one was pure army, even in civilian dress: shoulders back, eyes straight ahead, feet wide apart in parade stance. The faded yellow stripe down his pant leg was the only visual confirmation of his identity.

Blue finally broke the grinning silence. "Mister, I got me a problem you can help solve. My name's Blue Mitchell. Men in back of me, the Indian's name is Mickey, the other is one Vace Yarborough, lately of Tucson. Mickey and me, we got a confession of the truth in certain matters from Mr. Yarborough, and need a witness to his signing. Hoping you could oblige.''

It was pretty weak, not much of a story for a man to hang his decision on. Blue had gone over and over it, working at the words, but he could find nothing better than the blunt truth. The paper itself, when this man read it, told it all. A second look at the man let Blue know the truth was the only way.

"Why have you chosen to come to my camp? Surely you know that the Fort is not more than a day's ride from here, and you would find official witnesses there, and the law, ready to deal with you. Is that your reason for coming to me, the presence of the law?"

Blue nodded. "An Indian, name of Ketah, said to come here to you, that you were the one that would listen and help." He stumbled on the next words.

"The law wants me. For murder. And I got the proof that says no. Them two men, the Indian's been riding with me, the other can do the proving wrong. I don't want to be riding into a gathering of folks with an Indian beside me and a posted reader offering money on my head. Ketah said you were the man to help."

The last words were stuttered in a plea. Blue found himself battling to keep his gaze level, his eyes straight on the man with the questions. The nightmare sounded lame out here on the edge of the desert, in the brightness of daylight, with only one man asking questions, and another holding a rifle. He did not really know why he had come here, or what was special about this one man. Mickey had brought him here, and it was for him to play out the hand.

Blue sat straighter in the saddle, right hand going for the pistol on his hip. The rifle came up with him to steady its center as the guard leaned over to whisper a question to his commander. Blue felt the isolation of sitting high on the dun horse, a frightening vulnerability. He was wide open and exposed, at the mercy of the square-faced man and his aide. His belly rolled over, sending a sour taste flooding his mouth. The dun picked up his off hind foot to stand square and ready.

"Ketah is one of my scouts. Bring in your men and we will listen to the story."

The man turned away, exposing his wide back to Blue's handgun and temper. The guard stayed ready, watching Blue's hand, then let the rifle barrel drop away as the tall rider spun the dun horse and loped back to the two men waiting in the fold of the hill.

Mickey rode down to meet Blue, pulling the chestnut along, and paying no attention to the unwilling rider. Blue swung in beside the Indian, and the three returned to the comfort of the small camp. The fire was stirred to life, and the soldier was cooking something in the black iron pan. Coffee boiled on the coals.

This time the voice came from behind the shoulder of a dark red mule. "Light down, tie up here. Enough room on the line. We've got a bit of extra ration for your mounts. Looks to me they need it."

Blue settled gingerly into the shallow depression on his heels. Mickey squatted down just back of him, knife still in its sheath, shoulders relaxed, hands swinging free from his knees. Vace Yarborough was near them, tied with rawhide thongs to the thickest of the mosquite bushes. The straw-hatted man had the paper, and did not lift his head from the reading of it when the soldier wordlessly passed out cups of coffee. Blue welcomed having something to do with his hands, to take away the edginess of sitting still. He drank the coffee he did not want, and felt the bitter liquid stir in his belly.

Mickey must have felt the agitation, for the Indian put a hand to Blue's shoulder and pressed quickly, then raised his cup in a salute to the straw-hatted man who was still reading. Blue copied the gesture and forced himself to relax. They were at the mercy of this man, but Ketah said he was the one, and Mickey knew enough to believe his brother.

"This reads very clearly, Mr. Mitchell. But one question. How did you get this man out of Tucson? I don't need to ask the reason for the man's willingness to talk, but I would like to know about his abduction."

His eyes flickered from the impassive dark face of the Indian to settle on the odd ocean-green eyes of the young man. The paper he held in his fingers, with its awkward spellings and labored words, gave only part of the story. He was intrigued.

The story sounded unreal as Blue told of the long afternoon and evening he spent in Tucson, waiting for his opportunity to take Yarborough away from his safety and his companions. It was hard to match the older man's stare as he talked, and the words were sometimes slow in coming. But when he finished, the man slapped his knee in wonder, and laughed.

"It seems to me, Mr. Mitchell, that some of the time you have acted with less than good sense, but you have never lacked for guts, my friend. What do you plan to do with this Mr. Yarborough once I sign your document? You cannot just turn him loose, and the law will most likely grab you first if you enter the city with him in tow with only your word."

Blue shook his head. This man was way ahead of him everywhere he turned. "Been going one step at a time, sir." He found the title slipped out easily. Mickey grunted what sounded like agreement. "If I up and kill him, the law won't be satisfied, and I'll either hang or run. Can't turn him loose, and can't bring him to town on my own. Best to leave him with Mickey and sort it out with the law, then come back for him."

For the first time Vace Yarborough brought up his head and protested. He sat up against the pull of the rope around his neck and waved his bound hands.

"You can't leave me with that damned savage. He'll kill me first chance. Him and those two others. Be outright vicious to leave me with him." The absurdity of his words sank in, and Yarborough knew his defeat was complete. He sank back to his reclining position, face flushed, sweat beading across his forehead. His eyes shifted between the two men, never quite meeting their gaze.

The square-faced man spoke first; "There is a simpler and more humane solution. I can send him back to the fort under guard, which will free you to ride back and sort out your own skirmish with the law. Mickey may stay with us where he will be safe. You will only have your own safety to be of concern."

Blue did not have time to nod his acceptance. The gray whiskered man continued as if it were all planned. "My time is short. In a few days I will be leaving Arizona. Yesterday I watched the trains take away some of my enemies, and some of my friends. But there is time for me yet, and I can do this one more thing. All right, Mr. Mitchell, give me your prisoner and I will escort him back to the fort. But first, stay and eat dinner with us. There will be rabbit and beans ready in a few moments."

Two men had come to the camp, one carrying two Winchesters, one holding a brace of rabbit. They ignored the conference and went about their chores, and soon a good smell had grown from the cooking fire. Blue glanced at Mickey, ready to take his next move from him, but there was no need. The Indian was motionless on his heels; his hand moved in a vague circle of greeting. Mickey grinned at the worry he saw in the odd eyes. At times this one was too old.

"I need a pen, Wilson. And introduce these gentlemen to O'Donnell and Niebling. They will be joining us for dinner. Gentlemen." He sat on the convenience of a rock, and the document was signed with a flourish and handed back to Blue.

The relief that flooded him made the words sound thick and stupid. He stammered a thank you and worked at saying more.

"It is not over for you yet, my friend. You still have your ride into the city, and your confrontation with the law, as well as your search for the man named Adderson. It is not yet over. But please, do rest up and join us for dinner before you ride."

Blue walked past Mickey to the picketed horses. He stood by the dun and leaned his weight into the safety of the solid horse. Eyes closed, he rested in the familiar warmth of the animal's smell. Then he found his balance again, and opened his eyes. The document felt brittle in his hands, the words holding his life. He started rolling the paper, anxious to pack it safely and ride out. The bold signature across the bottom of the page read "George C. Crook."

★ Chapter 16

Tucson was getting itself civilized; even had a Chief of Police and deputies, no more dependence on a town marshal and a few rowdy gunslingers to keep the peace. One of these deputies, making his late-night rounds, walked into the flat out body of Bristol Adderson. Damning the drunks who thought they could sleep where they fell, he rolled the snoring man back into the side alley, cursing all the time his great bulk. The early morning darkness hid the swelling bruise that covered the side of his head.

There was a time, as he woke up, when Bristol could remember nothing—name, place, even the year. Who the hell was he and what in God's name was he doing sleeping in a pile of horse shit? He gagged at the sweetness of the crumbly texture filling his mouth, and rolled over to land in a fresher pile. Anger beat aside the pain in his head.

Then the curses started, and the familiar roll of the words juggled in his mind, bringing up a name, an extra face. Then the events of the night flooded him. Vace was gone. Some goddamned greaser got a hold of his horse and he was gone. Vace would 'a come back if he got free. Bristol

grabbed on to that fact, and built his memories around it.
Vace would come back for him.

He patted down his vest pockets, then stood to lean his
bulk on the coolness of the livery wall. Hands went over his
pants, seeking anything that would buy him another drink.
He ran his tongue around in his mouth, digging at the mush
imbedded in his teeth. Spitting dry did nothing; he had to
have whiskey to get cleaned out.

Goddamnit. The cursing started again. Not a dime on
him, not even a useless bastard penny. And no sign of Vace.

Bristol made it to the dim inside of the stable in a series of
staggering steps. The face and the voice that greeted him
were not what he wanted, and the cursing rivaled his own
efforts. Bristol stood flatfooted for the lecture that finally
ended with something he could understand. He didn't like
it, but it was something to hang on to for now.

". . . And you and that son-of-a-bitching partner of
yours, thinking you can ride out 'a here day and night, then
come stumbling back in the morning looking like a
strangled hound and wanting help. Well, I tell you mister, I
been talking to the police. They tell me what I can do with
deadbeats likes 'a you. You owe me two day's rent on them
broncs. That's four goddamn dollars 'merican. And you
gonna work off that money at a dollar a day, can sleep in the
loft or wherever you damned well find a bed. But you come
here and work, damn you, till your pard comes back with
them broncs. Or I get them policemen to set you up pretty in
jail."

There was more, mostly about his lineage and his
parents' doubtful marriage, and Bristol let it go right over
him. Wasn't nothing he ain't heard before. He knew there
was a place for him, where he could wait and watch for
Vace. The pinch-faced man's temper finally ran down,
settled by the string of words. He even had enough pity i
him to hand the smelly drunk a lukewarm cup of coff

before he put him to work. Horses don't wait for a man's head to clear before they dump on the barn floor. He handed over the three-tined fork and motioned to Bristol. Shovel from here to here, and get at it.

He knew now it had been a mistake to sit at the fire and take dinner with the General. Yet Mickey motioned for him to stay, to eat, and had accepted his own plate of the rabbit stew and beans, pushing aside the strangeness of the spoon to use his knife. Even Vace Yarborough had been untied and set down to eat. The neck rope stayed in place, insuring his finishing the meal with them.

Blue had been fascinated as he watched the whey-colored face catch the quick flash of Mickey's knife. The Indian shoveled in the beans and thick bits of stew. Vace Yarborough had to be thinking back to the dawn, and the painful tracks that same knife had made up into the privacy of his groin. He saw Yarborough clamp down on his lower lip and turn away, hand in midair, shaking the piece of rabbit free from the spoon.

Now Blue knew the same shaking. He rubbed his hand deep into his eyes. He had to stay awake, keep his mind alert. He could not count back to when he had slept. The hour of dozing before dawn had been his first time down in more than two days.

The dun took advantage of his rider's slowing responses, and stopped to tear into a palo verde, then wandered to a more tempting clump of grass. Blue let the horse stand and graze. There was something more important that had to be reasoned with and figured out. Damned if he could remember what.

Timing. The flat expanse of desert waved in heat as far as he could see. The soldiers behind him said the ride to Tucson was a long eight hours on a fresh horse. That made ɔ sense. It would put him into the city past midnight, right into the heart of the late-night drunken fights, with no guarantee he would find the law before it, or someone else, found him. It was so easy Blue started to laugh, spooked the dun, and found himself lying in a cactus looking up at the underjaw of the startled horse. He'd seen a picture of a camel once, something the army been playing around with; damned if the dun gelding didn't look like one of them cussed beasts from down here.

The laughter took over. Blue's shoulders rocked, his whole body gave in to the laughter that started to choke him. He grabbed the curious dun and found his balance to stand up.

Sleep. That was the answer to his timing problem. Life-giving, time-wasting sleep. A few hours now would put him in Tucson early morning. So obvious it had to jump up and grab him out of the saddle before he figured it out.

A twist in the dry wash, a tumble of rock near an overhang of exposed mesquite roots. No graze, but the dun had finished a nose bag at the campsite. Blue tied the reins to his boot, wadded his vest under his head, tilted his hat, and lay back. After a few minutes, the dun tugged at the restraint of the reins, cocked his head at the strange sounds coming from the long body, and lowered his head to rest.

There was only one horse. The brown gelding, walking in very slowly, keeping one foreleg off the ground in a hobbling, three-legged jump. Only one horse, led by a dark-skinned figure, black hair braided and wrapped in bright cloth. Only one horse, only one man.

She ran. Picked up the hem of her long skirt and she ran, straight for the Indian, feet hitting the hardpacked ground and leaving a trail of settling dust. The early sun blinded her; perhaps there was another horse, another rider yet out of sight.

"Mickey, where is he? Is he all right? What happened? Please. Don't tell me he's been hurt. Mickey."

The brown horse was sweated and dripping, his glossy coat turned a dull tan with the salt. Too tired and too sore to even pick up his ears at the flapping great skirt or the flailing arms, the brown gelding welcomed the chance to stand, and lowered his head until his muzzle almost touched dirt.

"He take piece of paper to Tucson to find law. He need help. You ride."

The trembling weakened the horse: legs shaking, side rippling in pain, neck bowed, knees beginning to buckle. Mickey felt the horse start to go down, and lashed at the animal with the reins, jerking hard on the bit, savaging the tender mouth to keep the horse from giving up.

"Miss, take stick and hit hard, keep horse moving. We get him to the ranch. I treat him. Hit harder."

It took five more long and impatient minutes for the hobbling brown to find the comfort of a soft-bedded shed. Five more minutes of Mickey's labored story. Celita did not wait to see her father's once-favored horse go down on its side in the sweetness of the cured winter grass. Mickey would heal the animal, or tend it until its death. It was now for her to get to Tucson.

"Mama, Mama." Her voice echoed in the morning darkness of the house. Celita skidded to a stop and listened. There was a series of soft noises in the small room from the kitchen, where Blue had lain for so long, where others had passed their burial night. It was here her mother had chosen to grieve alone.

"Mama, Blue's riding into Tucson. Mickey says he's got a paper proving he didn't kill Papa. I've got to help him."

There was a smile waiting for her as she came into the small room. A tentative smile, drawn from the lines of sadness.

"Yes, Celita. You must go to him, but go with a

calmness, not in panic. There will be trouble enough. Now tell me what Mickey has told you. And I will help you get ready. You must take him what he will have need of."

Her mother did nothing more than nod at the short tale retold by her daughter. She moved slowly through the house, listening while they pulled out a pair of pants, a tough canvas jacket, a faded shirt. It took a nail and a hammer to punch another two holes in the belt that would carry the holster around Celita's waist.

Mickey had a horse roped out and waiting, a tough blue roan standing barely fourteen hands, chosen to run the distance to the old mud walls of the town without effort. It was Ruth Maldinado who brought out the cartridge belt and the Winchester. Her daughter's small saddle gun would not do.

The fast-moving excitement kept Celita from thinking. She reacted to everything: the quickness of her mother's hands, the harsh nicker from the roan pony, the smell and feel of the unfamiliar weight of the gun and holster at her hip. It was when she slowed down to tie the smooth leather straps around the saddle bags that she knew what she was doing. And why.

Blue Mitchell. The feel of those long hands, the safety found in leaning against his chest, the look to those startling blue-green eyes. It was for him. Celita's hands stopped in midair, still holding onto the half-tied knot. She was afraid.

Her mother saw the fear, and wrapped a strong arm around her daughter.

"You are going for him, and he will be there for you when this is over. Go with him, child. Fight for him, and when it is over, tell him you love him. And go with my blessing . . . and that of your father."

There was no time for the tears. Celita hugged the sturdy body, holding on a long time, yet becoming impatient to ride. She slipped onto the roan's back and swung the little horse around in a high circle over his hocks. The blue horse bolted from the ranch, freed to run his heart out by the lightweight rider on his back.

Ruth Maldinado did not watch her daughter leave. She went to the small shed and the downed horse, to stand with the silent Indian and watch the labored breathing of the once-fine animal. She turned her mind away from the wild ride and the angry law in Tucson. There was nothing more she could do.

Clement Proctor was proud of his job, and scared of it. Chief of Police. A good title for a man to lay claim of. Had it less than a year and was still getting used to it. Hard to keep up with Buttner's reputation as a tough man. But Clement G. Proctor was getting a handle on the routine and making some of his own mark on the lawless in the city.

Routine was the answer. Like now, him sitting here at his desk before the rest of the town was moving, going over last night's reports, making his plans for the day. Not just letting things happen, but directing them. Hell, he even went over the new readers each morning, with his coffee, checking for faces he might need to know. Went over the old ones, too, reacquainting himself with those wanted by the law.

A lot of the bad ones drifted through Tucson, going on its reputation as a town easy on the lawless. Figuring it for a wide open town. No longer, not while Clement Proctor was the Chief of Police here.

He really liked that title.

The town was starting to move, mostly wagons still, coming in for supplies or moving goods through town. The barber shop would be opening in ten minutes; Proctor looked forward to getting a clean shave every day. He rubbed a smooth hand across the stubble. A good barbering would be the making of a man's day. He liked to think it was a symbol of the continuing civilization of Tucson.

Proctor's head turned. He could count the footsteps. Be at the door in four more beats. John Calder Hollenbeck; his deputy. Good man with a gun, short, powerful, John ran the office while the chief was getting his shave and testing the temper of the city. A good man, Hollenbeck, short on size and humor, but, by God, accurate with his gun.

Proctor stood up and pushed back the sturdy oak chair. One arm in his black frock coat, he nodded to the deputy and stepped around him to the street. He finished shrugging into the coat while he stood outside. Not good for the Chief to be seen walking the street in a mended vest and rolled up sleeves. He took a deep breath. It was going to be another good day.

★ Chapter 17

He liked a town this time of day. The streets were silent, the air clear of dust. A man could ride easy without bumping into seven more. In the three blocks he'd ridden so far, there had been only one person out walking. The bowed head had come up with unfocused morning eyes, and the half-turned flip of the hand became a salute between rider and citizen.

The tiredness was gone from Blue. Even the dun had an eagerness to his step that gave lie to the past eight hours of travel. Not hard running, but a steady trot that took in the miles. Even so, eight hours covered a lot of distance.

The closest he got to thinking things to a logical end was to hunt out the law real early, at gunpoint if necessary. Then force the law to read the paper and acknowledge it. Then he would get to Adderson. The man would probably stay in town without Vace, if he was up and moving from the merciful kick of the buckskin horse.

Blue crossed the main street, and knew the name of the street from the sign painted bright and clear and hanging from a gaslight post. There were more people now, hurrying to get somewhere fast. Blue found breathing difficult; any one of these good folk could look up at him and remember the description. He dropped his eyes, stopped looking around. Better off asking questions than running the risk of a whole mob seeing him.

There was one man not in a hurry. Wearing a clean black coat, looked formal, almost like an undertaker. A tall, clean-shaven man, clean everywhere. Bright white shirt, soft tan pants, and polished boots. A real good citizen. Only the pistol hung low at his hip gave Blue pause, but the man looked right at him and grinned his "good morning." Blue asked his directions and got sent down the street and to the right. Nice and polite. Blue tipped his hat in thank you.

There was a dark bay tied to the railing. A real solid horse, clean lines, good rigging, and a fancy new Winchester stuck in the scabbard. Guess the owner felt tying up in front of the law would protect his property. Blue tied the dun at the opposite end of the railing, and slapped the horse when a hoof came up to threaten his new neighbor.

Here it was. The office of the law. Only in this town it was called the Police Station. Still a jail, still the end to a man's freedom, and his life, if he guessed wrong. Blue hacked twice to clear his throat, and his right hand patted the precious folded piece of paper in the buttoned safety of his vest.

The man seated at the scarred desk looked the part. Wide shoulders, a heavy moustache covering his face, shirt frayed at the collar, with the badge of his profession pinned at an angle on his left pocket. He barely looked up, but did offer a grunt when Blue walked into the small office. Blue stayed on the near side of the close room; this was as far as he could force himself.

The smell was the same. Being in the Arizona territory didn't make this jail any different from the others Blue'd been in. He coughed again, looked to spit, then swallowed. The man behind the desk still did not look up.

Until Blue's hand went to his pocket and fumbled for the paper. Then the brown-capped head came up, and a hand grasped a small shiny revolver on the desk, hammer pulled back, barrel pointed at Blue. He read the sign; better get the explanation started before the law blew his head off. His sweat slicked the edges of the paper together and left Blue trying to pick them apart. He started talking.

"Says here, I'm Blue Mitchell, got a confession about the killing of Rafael Maldinado . . . "

There was no more time. The blocky man pushed back the chair and swung out beyond the desk, hand bringing up the short muzzle of the gun, aiming it directly at Blue.

"Got your nerve, mister. Give you that. Put up your hands and shuck that paper. You're wanted for murder. That's nothing a bit of paper'll change. Got the reader right here."

This wasn't right. Blue had made no threat to the man, had come on peaceful, gun holstered, rifle out on the dun. He held out the paper and tried again.

"This paper here proves . . . "

He took one step toward the man, waving the separated sheets that held the rest of his life.

"Mister, you put that damned paper down and step back, hands raised like I told you. Maybe then I'll look at your paper."

The pages fluttered to the desk top. Instead of reaching for them, the man dug into a desk drawer and brought out handcuffs. He tossed them across the desk to Blue.

"Put them on and turn around."

Blue looked at the bit of paper, lost on the official mess of reward dodgers, descriptions, and complaints littering the shiny oak. Hands bound in the metal cuffs, he would have no way of forcing the law to look at the paper, no way to defend himself. He hadn't come to Tucson to give up, but to fight. He bent down to pick up the cold metal, struggled with them and then looked at the law in confusion and held out the cuffs.

With a quick twist he threw them hard at the square face. At the same time he dove for the desk, frantic to get his hands on the paper. The deputy reached for the handcuffs out of instinct, the same instinct that made him pull the trigger.

The blast almost by the side of his head, deafened Blue. There was a momentary burn down his arm as he skidded across the desk, nose buried in paper. The deputy brought the small pistol up again, almost directly in front of Blue's face. He stepped back and slid on the metal cuffs. The gun fired again; the bullet tore into the adobe wall behind Blue.

Blue shoved from his boot toes and skated across the desktop, sending papers flying, and propelled himself into the solid man. They landed flat on the plank floor. The law's head hit the wood with a hollow thump, and Blue felt the body underneath him go limp. It was over before it got started. He sat back, knees on either side of the solid body, and swiped at the water collecting under his hat.

There were footsteps running outside, headed towards the small office. Many footsteps, voices yelling, men keyed up by the shooting. Blue was frantic. He dug through the mass of paper, desperate to find the two sheets. It was strange; as he rooted in the shifting piles, he saw bright red stains, some fresh enough to puddle before soaking into the paper fibers. He looked down at his arm where it burned, and wondered at the length of red showing through the dull blue of the sleeve. It confused him. He craned his head to look at the inside of his elbow. A dark gray circle was centered by a welling of blood. He'd been hit by the first shot.

There was no pain, and his fingers flexed when he trie them. Blue dropped to his knees to get at what he hop were his papers, and found the description of himself on the faded reader. No wonder the law was quick to shoot.

There it was, buried under last night's report. Blue rolled the two pieces together and stuffed them in his back pants pocket. He leaned over to pick up the loose gun. A quick check showed it was empty, and he threw it in the corner as hard as he could. It bounced and slid under a chair.

He was still waiting. He had heard the sounds of men running, recognized the wild yells that came right after the two shots. Then Blue put his head back and laughed. Tucson wasn't as civilized as the good folks would have it. The yelling was across the street, men gathering in a tight group to slap each other on the back. Either news of a gold strike or more about the Indians. The two shots from the office of the law had gone unnoticed.

It was simple to walk out the front door, close it gently, and turn right to walk away from the sleeping dun and the powerful-looking bay. The small group across the street had split up, some standing in twos and threes to talk eagerly. No one bothered with one more seedy-looking drifter. They were interested in their own news.

He stayed close to the buildings. If anyone was to pass him on the right, they could not help but see the red streaks down his arm. Pain began, slight at first, then bursting into a full bouquet. God almighty, it hurt. Let him know with each step he had to do something, and soon.

A warmth ran down into his palm, dripped off the ends of his fingers to spot the ground. Blue put his left hand at the top of his upper arm near his shoulder and found the crease, slick with blood. Sweat covered his forehead as he drew his fingertips down the arm, following the diagonal curve of the crease as it crossed his biceps to the inside of his elbow. The furrow was deeper there, and the fabric of the shirt was burned black. The law had been aiming at the top of his head as he dove across the desk. Blue shuddered.

It made no sense. He couldn't wander around Tucson looking like a victim of the Indian wars and waiting for a lawman to wake up and cry murder. He turned another corner, hesitated as the progression of storefronts seemed familiar. Halfway down the street, on the other side, was the dubious safety of Mr. Warner's Mercantile.

Wagons crossed in front of Blue. A man slammed into him and mumbled something that could be his manners or a curse. There was a ringing in Blue's ears, a distance between him and his legs. He couldn't stand here, yet there was a reason he could not walk across the street and into the calmness of the store. Another man bumped into him, jolted him hard, and Blue remembered, as the pain of his arm echoed behind his eyes. Blood. But he had to move on.

Soon someone would walk into the shambles of the law office and wake the stunned man. If Blue stood here like a poleaxed steer much longer, he might as well burn the papers and hang himself. Save the city the trouble.

A heavy ranch wagon started the turn down the street. Blue gauged his steps, and came off the walkway to fit in behind the wagon, then moved to the other side, walking close to the big, slow turning wheel. The driver didn't look back, but watched a too-well-dressed lady make her way so very carefully along the edge of the street.

Blue stayed with the wagon until it crossed paths with a high-stepping team of blacks. He followed their wake, angling closer to the invitation of the open door. One foot on the walk and he met eyes with a kid who looked back at him, then at his arm, and almost got his mouth open to scream. Blue growled at the child, a boy of no more than five. Growled fiercely to match the pain in his arm, and the panic driving him. The boy turned and fled into the skirts of his mother, who reached down absently and patted his head.

He walked into the store as if there were no blood on him,

no law after him, no crowd wanting him. Stepped into the
blessing of the dark walls shelved floor to ceiling, half-
empty now but holding a promise. He took the path he
remembered, the path the frantic bay gelding had slid along.
Past the steep railings of the stairway, careful to duck his
head at the right-angled supports, then through the unlocked
door into the storeroom.

Not until he closed the door behind him and stood for a
moment did he hear the voices. The clatter of his heeled
boots had blocked out the sound. A sweet sound like
Celita's voice. Blue shook his head, noted with disinterest
the droplets of blood that flipped from the ends of his fingers
and stained the white bags of new flour.

Celita. She looked up in the middle of her talking with
Mr. Warner and saw him. Swaying back and forth on the
uneven wearing of his boots, barely able to stand. The dust-
thickened light blotted his outlines, but she could see him. It
took only a quick word to Mr. Warner and she came to him,
walking with a measured grace, head high, eyes carrying a
private welcome. She walked to him like a woman grown,
with a dignity beyond her years.

Only three steps from Blue—close enough to see the
pleasure in his face, the tightness at his mouth, the pain
drawing his eyes—she became a child again. Her arms
came up as she skittered forward, and her head landed just
right, under his collarbone. Her arms went around him and
Blue did not feel their tightness against the burned muscle
of his wound.

He lost track of the time. Then Charlie Warner stood at
his shoulder, white rolls of cloth and an untopped wide-
mouth jar stacked in the crook of his arm. His other hand
was holding the back of a slatted chair. Warner put the chair
own hard; the echo of the small legs hitting the dusty floor
ught Celita's eyes back into focus.

Blue untangled the girl and turned to sit down, lost his balance in the spinning of his head, and felt the hardness of the caned seat slap his butt as he sat down. He shook his head at the distress in Celita's face.

"There's no time, girl. I left one of the police lying flat on his back in the office. Got to find one of the law around here willing to read a paper. Mighty important to me."

"Mickey told me about the paper. I'll help, Blue. So will Mr. Warner."

Blue jerked his arm away from the gentle hands and tried to stand. Celita put a hand to his chest and pushed.

"You set and let me talk. We've got it figured. Mr. Warner says that Clement Proctor is the chief, he's the one who might listen. He's the one we've got to find." Her face contorted into a frown. "Describe the man you fought, the one in the office. It can't be Mr. Proctor."

"Short, beefy, brown hair and whiskers. Wouldn't listen to whatever I said."

Warner interrupted. "Good, that's Hollenbeck. Proctor's a tall fellow, slicked-back hair and clean face. Usually over to the barber's this time of the morning."

He turned to the girl and handed her the wide-mouthed jar.

"You finish up here. The arm isn't bad, just messy. Your mother taught you well enough. I'm going to the barbershop. Mitchell, you give me the paper and be here when I get back. This will be the safest place in town for you. Time Hollenbeck comes to, the whole town'll be buzzing with your name and planning on spending the reward. Liable to potshot you just walking back to the police station. You set right here."

God, Warner talked a lot when he got going. Blue fingered the folded square of paper, then looked in Warner's face and handed the man the priceless bit of pap

Then Warner was gone, hat placed squarely on his thinning hair.

Celita put two fingers to his lips and shushed him gently, not letting Blue get his feet under him. Leave it to Mr. Warner, she said. And then she took the long-handled scissors and picked at the top of the torn sleeve, dragging it away from his shoulder. Blue felt the coolness of the air ruffle the fine hair on his arm as the blades stroked clean. The only sign of her distress was the almost silent intake of breath as Celita peeled the material away, starting at the top, lifting each thread of the stained cotton as it stuck to his flesh.

Blue tried to match her breath for breath, holding his as she worked the unraveled bit of cloth from the exposed white edge of his muscle, easing out the tension to get ready for the next tug. He wanted desperately to reach forward and touch his mouth to the fine sweat at her hair line, to somehow take from her the pain she was holding. His arm was numb, as if she had absorbed the fire.

Then she caught her lower lip in her teeth and warned him with her averted eyes. The smell gagged him before the flash burned down into his belly, tearing at him in a wheeling of pain. He refused the offer of a deadening drink, just shook his head and turned his face away. He was not capable of words. If he opened his mouth now, it would be to scream. The whiskey burned its path down his arm, and washed a clean, cold path to his fingers. Then the fire died to an icy burn.

The smell of the salve was familiar to him, and welcome. Pine tar, turpentine, linseed oil. A good concoction to heal any open sore on a horse, to keep away flies and infection. Celita used the salve's oily thickness to fill in the tunnel dug y the bullet, gently patting the evil smell level with the touched flesh of his arm. The bandage wound around the upper arm put a strength back in his arm, as if he could feel the repair and lean into the support.

Celita leaned down and kissed him. Quickly, on the mouth. Then stood back to admire her work.

"Miss, I got to get to Adderson. Been thinking over Mr. Warner's words. If Bristol hears I hit town, he'll run. And I owe him too much to let him go now. He's the one fired on your pa. Get me a gun, I'm going after him."

He saw the look in her eye. He knew it, from the first day he rode the bay gelding against her wishes. Blue stood and took one step toward the girl; she backed up one step. He tried one more step, and she moved away from him again.

"Miss. I thank you again. You're kind to help, to be here. But I got to . . ."

"And you haven't learned a thing. Adderson's a bully. He'll beat you to a pulp or . . . Damn it, he's more than you can take."

They were both shocked by her words. Blue liked her caring. No one ever cried for him before.

"Me and Bristol, we go back a long way. I got a sign on him and he knows it. All I need to do is find him and he'll run right into my fist. He's too close now to let go."

Blue shrugged his right arm, smiled at the numbed throbbing. "You did a good job here, don't feel a thing. This won't slow me down none."

It was a lie; the slight movement woke a warning spasm through his shoulder and back. Blue widened his smile, remembering how it felt to grin at his enemies and watch the anger draw past their common sense.

Then the insolence came back full term to match the sureness of his words. Damn it, he had a fixed arm, a letter turning him free, and an old grudge to settle with the fat-faced son who'd roped him and hog-tied him to be sho

"He got your pa, miss. I can't let that go."

Blue looked down at his hands, spread the ten fingers wide, and flexed them, made two fists. He would not admit to the line running up to his shoulder. The hands worked, and that was all he needed for now.

He could take Bristol Adderson.

★ Chapter 18

It felt good. Have to tell Rosa how good it felt. To be doing something again, not the kind of doing where he stood behind the counter and measured dusty fabric or shoveled out dried beans by the pound. The anger and the ever-present need for a drink were gone, replaced by a lightness inside that pleased him.

Warner ran his fingers through the thick growth of brush at his jowls. Chief Proctor had a good idea, keeping clean shaven, and doing it every day; put a sense of duty and honor back in a man. Maybe after this fracas was over, he'd take himself to the barber, get the vegetation trimmed to a respectable quarter-inch. Warner's step quickened. Right now he needed to find the law, and fast.

He stayed on the opposite side of the police station, almost skipping his steps in his hurry to turn the corner and see the wide painted stripes of the barber pole. The growing cluster of men who'd been yahooing their celebration earlier had shifted sides of the street, and more were ganging around the half-open door. Damn. That meant Hollenbec was discovered and the word was out.

One man detached himself from the group, angled a path across the busy street, and came to the walkway almost at Charlie's back. Charlie acted on his impulse and stopped suddenly, forcing the man to walk into him. He turned and spread his arms in abject apology and held onto the man, patting him as if to look for damage.

"Why, sir, I am most apologetic, how rude of me to bump you so. There is no excuse for my behavior."

For a moment Charlie Warner forgot his mission and enjoyed his part, overwhelming the man with verbose kindness. Confusion blanked the pale eyes of the shambling drifter as Charlie spun a profusion of words and pats that would not allow the man to continue his hurried errand.

"Is there anything I can do to show the depths of my feeling at this untimely interruption? Why I'm on my way to the barbershop, but I can take more than a few minutes to repay you for the abject rudeness of my treatment of you." Careful there, Charlie, my boy, you are overdoing this.

The man's voice fit his condition; gravel rough and hard spoken. "I ain't cared nothing for your fussings, mister. Headed for the law down to Ansel's cutting shop. Got to get him out 'a there and back to his jail. Hell, some outlaw come in and bashed the stuffings out 'a his deputy. Got to find the law and get out looking. There's a reward out for this 'un, and I fancy to get it."

"Why, my good man, I'm headed right now for Ansel's barbershop. Be delighted to bring back your law for you and let you get started on your search for the desperado. Be most delighted to help."

Suspicion over the flow of words warred with greed. The chinless man snorted at Warner's offer, then spat into the street.

"You tell Proctor that Hollenbeck's down, got a lump the e of a horseapple back of his head. Was that killer,

Mitchell, done it. One that shot the mex a while back. He'll know."

Right enough the chief of police would know. Charles Warner would make certain the man knew everything. Charlie patted the folded papers buttoned into his inside coat pocket. The lift came back to his steps as he left the manhunter under the gently swinging sign of the news vendors. LOCAL AND FOREIGN PAPERS FOR SALE. Tomorrow Charles Warner and company would be the news.

Ansel's wonderfully striped sign was easy to find. Warner elbowed inside and found the chief almost asleep.

"Chief Proctor, my name is Charles Warner. I have come on an errand of mercy. There is something I wish you to read that has a great deal of importance to you and to a certain young couple. Please, there is no need to interrupt your shave. . . . I can take the liberty of reading the document to you and then you may see it for yourself. If you will allow . . ."

He stumbled some in his reading, awkward with the half-mad spellings and smudged print. But the story came to the law with its treachery and greed clear and loud. Charlie Warner kept reading, slowing the words as he came to the end, knowing that the law was waving aside the ministrations of the barber to come erect in the padded comfort of the chair, eyes wide, mouth pursed in a gentle, wondering whistle. The reading made for a good story.

Even Charlie took in a deep breath as he read the signature of the witness. The kid hadn't said anything about this. Charlie knew the importance of this particular signature; there could be no doubting the veracity of the tale, not with this man as witness. His head jerked up from the dark scrolling of black ink that flourished across the bottom of the second page. The Chief's tuneless whistle became loud exclamation of disbelief.

"Let me see that, mister. Damned if it reads true." But the willingness to believe was strong in the half-lathered face. Charlie gave him the paper, gave him a minute to run his eyes over the two wrinkled sheets, to study the lines of the well-known signature.

"The boy's in town right now, Chief. He's had a fight with your deputy, Mr. Hollenbeck. Who, I gather, would not listen to him and tried to put him in your fine jail.

"There is a mob out hunting for the boy right now, spurred on by the meager offering of $50. They know he is in town, and will shoot to kill without mercy. What they don't know is that, right now, he is in my storeroom with the young woman whose father he is supposed to have killed. She has never believed the story, and came to help him."

God, Charlie, say what you got to and let go. The boy's life is getting shorter and shorter and you're interrupting his chances with your damned words. Charlie swore at himself; it was hard changing the habits of a long lifetime.

"Chief, come to my store. Then you and the boy can walk back to your office, him in your custody. No one will fire on him. Then you can spread the word. Come with me now."

Clement Proctor had reached the door before the shop-keeper had finished his story. The soap drying on his face itched, and the bristly hair cut from around his ears dug sharp points into his neck. All that could wait. Now he had to catch up with Mitchell and get him out from the mob. Adderson and Yarborough being mixed up in this didn't surprise him at all. And he wished to God that Warner for once would shut up.

The narrow alleys and close-set houses were his best ance. But where to start looking? Blue eased his back against the clay wall and pulled his hat down over his eyes. Start where he'd seen Bristol last, the north end livery.

The clean shirt and borrowed frock coat gave him some protection, some blurring of his identity. It was hard just the same to walk the street in the open without seeing an enemy in each doorway or slow-ambling cowhand. There were some who slowed down as they came past him, eyeing Blue like a bronc up for sale. The sweat dripped down his back, his right arm throbbed, but Blue fumbled for something in his coat pocket, kept his head turned, and walked an easy pace, fighting the hurry in his mind by drawing a slow grin on his face. He had to find Bristol Adderson.

The rounded shoulders, the sloping set to the thick-muscled back gave the man to him. Bent over a steaming pile of manure, Bristol Adderson was heaving his gut into the mound, getting rid of last night's whiskey. Blue figured this made them even: Bristol's belly and his arm. He didn't wait to add up the handicap and read them to the public.

Just one word. A shout. "Bristol."

The man's head came up, saliva stringing from his slack mouth. Adderson was a dumb brute but there was no hesitation in him. He roared into Blue, spittle flying, hands reaching to end the torment. Blue obliged the man. He ducked under the reaching arms and rammed a doubled fist into the soft belly. Bristol bent with the force and stumbled, but came back faster than Blue figured.

A fist caught him in the arm, high up, almost at his shoulder, spinning him into the barn door and bringing him to one knee. Adderson's follow-up blow hit the wood above Blue's head, splintering the board and drawing a howl from the man. Blue came up under his arms and drove a hard left to the ribs, then crossed with a right under his chin.

That was a mistake. The damaged right arm muscle spasmed, turned numb, drew his fingers into a tight kno Adderson choked out an oath that fouled Blue's face, th reached his spread hand to grip Blue's arm. Blue fought against the hold and missed the right hand aimed at his face, taking the blow across his cheek. Adderson's left arm came back in a straight line, elbow jamming into the split flesh of his face hard enough to send lights through Blue's eyes.

That released the numbness. Blue drew his left back and short-armed Adderson in the gut. Once, twice, in quick succession. The clamp abandoned his right arm before Blue was steady and he lurched away from the support. His third blow to Adderson's belly met fleshy ribs with a wild impact as the man turned away from the attack. The unexpected force drove him to his knees, as Blue slammed sideways into the broken door.

There were voices. Full of anger, coming at him. Blue shook his head at the wonder of it and turned back to Adderson. The full force of the door caught him in the back, bowled him into his enemy, and brought them both to the softness of the manure-covered ground.

He didn't hear the curses coming at him, didn't know the face of the small man that opened in surprise, or see him run back into the barn. Adderson's face was what he could taste. He planted a fist on the offending nose and gloried in the bursting color of the red shower. The right hand was strong enough to hold onto the whisker-roughened neck. His left hand came back repeatedly to dance across the shattered nose, draw blood and flesh from the wide-angled hairiness above the dark eyes.

He knew Adderson's knees came up in a furious attempt to stop him, could feel their impact at his back, and allowed a grunt to escape, but he was not turned from his slaughter of the man's face.

He did know the broom handle that slammed him from Adderson's body. Blue rolled with the force of the blow, felt a weightless freedom until he hit the torn muscles in his right arm. That pain slowed him and opened his mind to what was going on above him.

"He's mine, I got the dirty killing son of a bitch. That fifty is mine."

Then a differing opinion offered in similar language.

"You ain't got him. He's mine, this here's my barn and he's mine. Don't . . ."

There was a thud, and then heavy breathing. Blue was surprised to find it was his own breath. Then it started again. Higher and wilder this time. More entrants into the grab for the prize. Blue Mitchell. Blue wanted to grin.

"That there killer belongs to me, got my gun on him now . . ."

"You be wanting the same slam to your head, can oblige any time, he's mine. . . ."

There were more, all claiming him, none with much imagination in their declaration. Blue wondered idly where Adderson had gone to, thought to roll his eyes open to look, but decided it wasn't worth the trouble.

Then things began to change.

"Chief, I got here first, knocked the bastard down, he's . . ."

"My stable, my hired man he's been walloping, he belongs . . ."

"Look out you greedy so-and-so, I can take you any time. This one's . . ."

Kind of funny, all these folks wanting him. Must be what it's like to be popular. Blue guessed he'd as soon be by himself. He finally opened his eyes.

There was a man standing over him, legs wide apart, sawed-off shotgun hanging at his side held with a strong hand. Kind of overkill, Blue figured. He wasn't going to fight anyone enough to need killing with such a weapon. He grinned up at the man, who looked down with a puzzled face.

The clean face was familiar to Blue. He thought on it, then remembered. The man he'd asked directions from earlier this morning. Seemed a long time ago.

Blue rolled his head in the dirt, spitting at the dryness on his tongue, and discovered a metallic taste of something warm sliding down his cheek into the corner of his mouth. Damn, he was beginning to hate the taste of blood. The voices continued their arguing over his head.

"Silence."

The word came in a roar accompanied by the skyward blast of the sawed-off shotgun. Blue gladly shut his mouth and kept his words to himself. The rest of the swelling crowd reacted in the same way. The quiet was a blessed relief.

Blue looked for Bristol Adderson, rolling his head from side to side. He finally found the man, flat out on his back, snoring with a flourish of bubbles through the flattened nose. Blue felt a pride in that reshaping; looked good on the sleeping man. He sighed deeply and found a deep bruised rib that objected. He finally looked up, beyond the long legs of the man holding the smoking shotgun.

Charlie Warner was there, a grin splitting his face into whiskered halves. He was standing with the long-legged man, close enough to crawl in the pocket that held the man's badge of office. Then there was the somber face of the girl. Celita. Black hair pulled into wild drawn braids, freckles strong against the paleness of her skin.

Blue smiled at her and tried to sit up. His right arm wouldn't take him and he lay back in the dirt. The smile let more blood into his mouth, and he coughed out the bitter taste, but kept the grin.

"You know, today is my birthday."

Celita couldn't help but return his grin. The puzzlement on the law's face was payment enough for the nonsense words.

Blue set himself once more against the threatened protest of bruised muscle and stood, to balance on widespread legs. He took one step forward. Celita followed, fingers digging into his flesh as she struggled to match his stride. The grin on Blue's bony face widened; it was all his now.

William A. Luckey was born in Providence, Rhode Island, but later went West to work with horses. "I've spent the past forty years dealing with rogue horses using my own methods to retrain and make them useful—I've evented, shown dressage, fox-hunted for twenty seasons, worked cattle, gone on five-day trail rides. I've owned over 150 horses personally, going back to when I was seven. I've actually been riding now for almost sixty years, and have taught riding for over forty years." *High Line Rider* appeared in 1985, the first of twelve Western novels published to date. William A. Luckey's most recent works are *The English Horses* (2007), and its sequel, *Burn English* (2008). Tense suspense and human drama characterize all of the Luckey Western stories and have constantly pleased readers worldwide.